Praise for *USA TOD...*
Merlin...

"Merline Lovelace rocks! Like Nora Roberts,
she delivers top-rate suspense with great
characters, rich atmosphere and a crackling plot!"
—*New York Times* bestselling author Mary Jo Putney

"Ms...
sto...

—...*Book Reviews on Wrong Bride, Right Groom*

★ ★ ★

Dear Reader,

Sooner or later, every exotic locale or intriguing historical site I visit ends up in a book! Our recent trip to Saint Petersburg was no exception. I fell in love with that city of beauty and White Lights. The gloriously restored Amber Room particularly fascinated me, as did the mystery surrounding the disappearance of the original.

So of course I had to send two intrepid OMEGA agents on the hunt for one of Russia's most priceless treasures. Hope you enjoy their wild chase and this glimpse into the world of missing art.

For updates of my latest travels and new books, be sure to check my website at www.merlinelovelace.com or join me on Facebook.

Merline Lovelace

MERLINE LOVELACE

Double Deception

ROMANTIC
SUSPENSE

Recycling programs
for this product may
not exist in your area.

ISBN-13: 978-0-373-27737-7

DOUBLE DECEPTION

Books by Merline Lovelace

Harlequin Romantic Suspense

†*Diamonds Can Be Deadly* #1411
†*Closer Encounters* #1439
†*Stranded with a Spy* #1483
†*Match Play* #1500
†*Undercover Wife* #1531
†*Seduced by the Operative* #1589
†*Risky Engagement* #1613
†*Danger in the Desert* #1640
†*Strangers When We Meet* #1660
†*Double Deception* #1667

Harlequin Desire

†*Devlin and the Deep Blue Sea* #1726
The CEO's Christmas Proposition #1905
The Duke's New Year's Resolution #1913
The Executive's Valentine's Seduction #1917

Harlequin Nocturne

Mind Games #37
**Time Raiders: The Protector* #75

†Code Name: Danger
*Holidays Abroad
**Time Raiders

MERLINE LOVELACE

A career Air Force officer, Merline Lovelace served at bases all over the world, including tours in Taiwan, Vietnam and at the Pentagon. When she hung up her uniform for the last time, she decided to combine her love of adventure with a flair for storytelling, basing many of her tales on her experiences in the service.

Since then, she's produced more than eighty action-packed novels, many of which have made *USA TODAY* and Waldenbooks bestseller lists. Over eleven million copies of her works are in print in thirty countries. Be sure to check her website at www.merlinelovelace.com for contests, news and information on future releases.

To Neta and Dave

Al and I treasure your friendship and all the great adventures we've shared—including that fabulous evening at Catherine Palace!

Chapter 1

Nick Jensen, code-named Lightning, took the call while attending a noisy, exuberant Fourth of July party at the MacLean, Virginia, home of Maggie and Adam Ridgeway. One of Washington, D.C.'s, true power couples, the Ridgeways were on a first-name basis with presidents and prime ministers, ambassadors and news anchors. They also sat on the boards of a half dozen charities that administered to the desperate needs of millions around the world.

The guest list at this particular party, however, didn't include the rich and famous. Instead, they'd limited it to the members of a small, very elite organization and their families. Nick's wife and twin boys formed one of the boisterous teams tossing water darts in the shallow end of the pool. Maggie and Adam's adopted grandchildren, Young Tau and Mei Lin, had roped their father into anchoring a second team. A very pregnant, very glowing Claire Cantrell Esteban, code name Cyrene, watched their antics from a shaded lawn chair. Maggie and Adam's equally pregnant eldest daughter Gillian kept Claire company.

As his gaze roamed the crowd, a fist seemed to reach into Nick's chest and grab his heart. These people were his life, the family he'd never had. He couldn't imagine a more different world from the one he'd roamed as a skinny, half-starved twelve-year-old. The backstreets of Cannes seemed a thousand light-years away.

As if reading his mind, the woman who'd rescued him from those streets wove through the picnic tables and slipped a hand through the crook of Nick's arm. "Our ranks keep growing, don't they?" Her smiling eyes lingered on the two pregnant women. "Literally and figuratively."

Nick glanced down at the now-retired operative he'd once offered to pimp for. Damned if Maggie Sinclair couldn't still command that kind of highly specialized service. Her brown eyes glowed with the vitality she brought to everything she did and her sparkling personality still made folks sit up and take notice whenever she walked into a room.

"Speaking of our ranks growing…" Nick tipped his chin toward a twosome engaged in a mock duel.

A diminutive, curly haired Xenia, queen of the

universe, swung her plastic laser sword. Adam Ridge-way II countered her thrusts with barbecue tongs. As tall and broad-shouldered as his father, Adam had inherited his mother's quicksilver grin and irrepressible sense of humor. He'd earned the nickname Tank on his own. Even as a small child, he exhibited a tendency to charge headlong into any and every situation. A Harvard law degree, a stint as Navy JAG and his current job as an assistant district attorney had tempered that tendency—but not his energy or thirst for new challenges.

He was up for another new direction, one that involved Nick and the woman standing beside him. Bracing himself for her reaction, Nick turned to Maggie.

"You know Tank came to see me yesterday, right?"

Most of Washington's elite recognized him as the President's Special Envoy. The largely honorific position had been created years ago as a reward for wealthy campaign contributors. Only a handful of trusted insiders knew the Special Envoy also served as director of OMEGA, an agency so secret it wouldn't be found on any government organizational chart.

Nick wasn't the only one at the party to carry the dual titles and heavy responsibilities. Both Maggie and her husband had headed OMEGA after spending time as field operatives. Their eldest daughter, Gillian, had also joined the ranks, but the acquisition of a ready-made family during her first op had limited her undercover activities. All three knew firsthand the dangers inherent in those ops, however. So Nick wasn't surprised at the small sigh that preceded Maggie's reply.

"Tank told us he'd talked to you."

"With his training and background, he's a natural." He waited a beat, two. "So will you carve me into bite-size pieces if I welcome him to our ranks?"

"According to Tank, there's no 'if' about it."

The tart response produced a wry grin. "Okay, I admit it. I want him. Unless you or Adam say otherwise, I'd like to have him understudy as controller on the next op."

"It's your decision." Maggie's glance lingered on her son. "And his."

"Then I'll…" A low but very distinctive ping from his cell phone cut him off. "Sorry. I need to take this."

She nodded her understanding. She'd been on the other end of enough calls from the president to understand the urgency. She watched Nick turn away to take the call, saw his shoulders stiffen as he transitioned into full Lightning mode. With a small sigh, she knew he would have to leave the party—and would take her son with him.

Twenty minutes later, Lightning pulled his JAG into his reserved spot in front of an elegant brick town house in the heart of D.C.'s embassy district. He and Tank emerged from the low-slung sports car and mounted the steps to the crimson-painted door with easy strides that belied their tension—Lightning's came from knowing he was about to send one or more of his operatives into the field, Tank's from finally becoming part of the organization that was in his blood.

The elegantly appointed offices of the Special Envoy occupied the town house's first two floors. OMEGA's ultra high-tech Control Center took up the third. Since the downstairs offices were closed in honor of the Fourth of July, Nick and Adam headed straight for the concealed elevator that whisked them up to the Control Center.

The epicenter of OMEGA thrummed with activity. Communications techs monitored message traffic at two consoles on one side of the room. A former CIA analyst peered at satellite imagery on the other. Lightning nodded to them by way of greeting and went directly to the agent manning the center console.

"You know Adam Ridgeway, don't you?"

"Sure do." Clint Black, code-named Blade, thrust out a hand. "How's it going, Tank?"

Blade's greeting was polite enough but he gave his boss a quick, questioning glance. Civilians, even one with this man's background and credentials, weren't normally admitted to the upper sanctum.

Lightning explained the apparent security breach with a brief announcement to the room at large. "Adam—Tank—is joining OMEGA."

After a round of back-slapping and congratulations from the on-duty crew, Lightning took a seat at the console positioned to give full view of the wall-size screens. The screen on the left contained a world map with glowing amber lights denoting the location of active OMEGA agents. Only one light was illuminated at the moment, indicating an agent currently in deep cover. The screen on the right provided the status and locale of operatives not in the field.

Blade used the center screen to update his boss. He'd been busy since Lightning's call less than a half hour ago. A click of a mouse brought up a digitized copy of a driver's license.

"This is Vivian Bauer, age thirty-four, current residence Arlington, Texas. According to the entry she posted on her Facebook page, she's in the process of cleaning out her grandfather's attic following his death last month. The grandfather was Thomas Bauer, eighty-nine, retired high school football coach."

Another image flashed up on the screen, this one of a tired-eyed, stubble-cheeked soldier in a WWII helmet and uniform.

"Bauer served with the 45th Infantry Division in Europe from April 1943, to July 1945. And this—" Blade brought up a third image "—is the item Bauer's granddaughter claims to have found with his old uniform and service ribbons in a trunk in his attic."

Lightning leaned forward, his eyes narrowing on a small round mosaic in varying shades of yellow. At the center of the mosaic were the curled petals of a rose.

"Bauer's Facebook entry generated a spate of comments," Blade related. "Mostly condolences on her grandfather's death. Then came this one from Dr. Renee

Dawson, professor of Art History, New York University."

The professor's input was brief. Only two lines. But her comment that the rose medallion looked very similar to one from a panel of Russia's famous Amber Room had triggered an instant reaction in the White House.

As the president had reminded Lightning during their brief conversation less than an hour ago, he'd recently had to arm-twist the Senate into ratifying a nuclear arms reduction treaty with Russia that had been decades in the making. He didn't want anything jeopardizing what both sides hoped would be a new era in international relations.

"The president's not too thrilled with the possibility that a U.S. serviceman may have had a piece from one of Russia's lost national treasures in his possession. It could prove an embarrassment."

Tank gave a low whistle. "More than an embarrassment. The Department of Justice is still working the fallout from the Hungarian Holocaust survivors' lawsuit settled a few years ago."

Lightning picked up on the comment immediately. "Wasn't that the suit involving the Treasure Train?"

"It was. The survivors alleged the U.S. Army mishandled millions of dollars worth of their property confiscated during WWII. The DOJ settled to the tune of twenty-five million in reparations."

A former army grunt, Blade didn't appreciate this

slur on his service. But it was hard to dispute the facts that had come out during the much-publicized lawsuit.

Fact: the pro-Nazi Hungarian government had confiscated the equivalent of billions of dollars worth of gold, jewelry, Persian carpets, artwork, cameras, silver cutlery and other valuables from Jews prior to sending them to concentration camps. Fact: German troops had loaded the looted property into boxcars for shipment to Berlin in the last, chaotic days of the war. Fact: American forces had discovered the infamous Gold Train hidden inside a cave in Austria.

After U.S. authorities decided they had no way to properly identify and return the thousands upon thousands of confiscated items, they transferred the train's contents to the International Refugee Organization. The IRO subsequently auctioned the items to provide relief for Jewish refugees and displaced persons.

Unfortunately, some of the looted items found their way into the offices and residences of senior U.S. military officers. Worse, robbers broke into the warehouse where the Gold Train contents were stored. Although some of the thieves were caught, prosecuted and punished, only a small portion of the stolen property was ever recovered.

So after decades of wrangling, the Hungarian Holocaust survivors sued the U.S. government on the grounds that it had failed to adequately protect their property. As Tank just pointed out, the settlement cost the DOJ a big chunk of change.

Now the U.S. faced the possibility that another of its WWII-era soldiers might have had stolen loot in his possession—this time from a long-lost Russian national treasure worth billions in today's currency. If so, the situation could put a decided dent in Russian/U.S. relations.

"I want you on a plane to Dallas within an hour," Lightning instructed Blade. "You and Rebel."

The operative's expression didn't change but OMEGA's director knew him well enough to detect the ripple just under his skin.

"Rebel pulled a tour as Assistant Air Attaché in Moscow during her Air Force days," Lightning reminded him. "She still has contacts that might prove useful."

Blade grunted an assent. So the woman rubbed him the wrong way at times? Okay, most of the time. They were both pros and they worked well together when they weren't scraping on each other's nerves.

"I'll call in Dodge to work with Tank as your controller," Lightning added. "He's got some useful contacts in Moscow, too."

He should, since he'd recently married an icily gorgeous Russian colonel.

Relieved that he'd have both Dodge *and* Tank watching his back, Blade contacted Vivian Bauer. She was surprised and a little wary to receive a call from a government official but agreed to an early evening meeting.

That done, he grabbed the file of data he'd hastily pulled together. He thought about hitting up OMEGA's Field Dress Unit for a sport coat but decided his jeans, black T-shirt and denim shirt with the sleeves rolled up would do in the summer heat.

He did stop by OMEGA's armory, though, to secure additional clips for his automatic. With the Sig nestled in its ankle holster and the bone knife he'd had crafted to his exact specifications in its leather sheath, Blade headed for Andrews Air Force Base.

He'd just parked and swung out of his pickup when Victoria Talbot, code name Rebel, roared up on her latest toy. The Ducati S2R had a max speed of 300 mph and a clutch as smooth as Irish cream. Or so Rebel claimed.

She spun to a halt less than two feet from where Blade stood and threw up a cloud of dust that made his jaw tighten. It torqued another notch when she heeled the aluminum side stand and swung off the bike. She'd come right from the Ridgeways' Fourth of July party, so she wasn't wearing her usual protective leather. Her scoop-necked red tank and thigh-hugging jeans might not have deflected many bugs but they skimmed her tall, slender form in a way that made his throat go dry.

"I called ahead," she said as she dropped the Ducati's keys into the envelope-style purse slung across her chest. From past ops, Blade knew the slim pouch held her weapon and communications device, along with tools that could transform her from biker babe to dewey-eyed coed with a few swipes of lip gloss and eyeliner.

"They're revving up a T-39 for us," she informed him airily. "You can brief me on the situation when we're in the air."

"I can, huh."

Ignoring the sardonic reply, she started for Base Operations in her hip-swinging, long-legged stride. Blade trailed behind and tried without notable success to keep his eyes off her jeans-covered butt.

Iridescent waves of aviation fuel shimmered above the hot tarmac. Rebel sucked in its stink greedily and wondered how many missions she'd flown out of Andrews while assigned to the Presidential Support Squadron. A hundred? Two? Wishing to heck she could be at the controls of the sleek executive jet sitting in its chocks, she led the way into Base Operations and out to the aircraft. The pilot was in the cockpit, the copilot waiting at the hatch. She didn't recognize the young captain but he recognized her.

"Good to finally meet you, Major Talbot. I've heard a lot about you."

"All lies," she countered, grinning.

He laughed and waited for his passengers to buckle in before providing an update on weather and fuel. "We're estimating two hours fifteen minutes flying time."

Rebel nodded. "That's how I figured it."

"Now for the civilians on board..."

The young captain shifted his attention to Blade for

the required safety briefing. When he was done, he swung back to Rebel.

"I gotta ask. Did you really tell the Air Force Academy Superintendent he must have crawled out from under a rock back in the Pleistocene Age?"

"I'm pretty sure I didn't use those precise words."

"But you did refuse to submit to some of the more sexist forms of hazing."

"Actually, I refused to submit to any form of sexist hazing."

"Nothing's changed there," Blade murmured as the captain went forward.

Rebel shifted in her seat to regard Clint Black. He returned her look with a bland one of his own, but she knew he was thinking of their titanic clash during her first week at OMEGA.

Black had been kidding around with two other agents. Didn't have a clue OMEGA's newest recruit was in the vicinity. Or that she would prove so damned touchy when he wondered aloud whether she had the training and/or skill to take down two hundred plus pounds of raging male. She'd smiled sweetly, batted her lashes and proceeded to toss him on his ass.

They'd put the incident behind them. They were both too professional not to. But memory of the thud when he hit the floor still gave Rebel a private chuckle. What didn't amuse her was that she couldn't quite forget how Black's lean, hard body had felt when she flipped it over hers.

She'd tried. God knows, she'd tried. The last thing she intended to do was get involved with someone in the same outfit. Especially someone who attracted women like junkyard dogs attracted fleas. She'd done that once, with disastrous results, and wouldn't make the same mistake twice.

Her divorce wasn't the primary reason she'd opted to leave the Air Force and take Nick Jensen up on his offer to join OMEGA, but it had certainly factored into the decision. At times she missed the military and the thrill that came with piloting multi-million-dollar jets. But only at times. Her civilian job as an adjunct instructor at the National Defense University and her missions for OMEGA kept her hopping.

Like now. Shoving aside the annoying thoughts of ex's and hard bodies, she got down to business. "All right. Tell me why we're on our way to Texas."

"We have an appointment with a woman named Vivian Bauer."

"Because?"

"Because Ms. Bauer recently cleaned out her deceased grandfather's attic and found what an NYU art history professor thinks may be a piece of the Amber Room."

Rebel jerked upright in her seat, eyes wide. "The Amber Room? The one some Prussian king gave Peter the Great back in the 1700s?"

"That's it."

"Holy crap!"

"Yeah, that seemed to be the general consensus."

He filled her in on what he knew, then passed her the file he'd assembled.

"Here's what we've got so far."

They touched down at an Air National Guard base on the outskirts of Dallas. A hot, muggy Texas evening instantly enveloped them, made to feel even hotter by the last rays of the blazing ball of the sun reflected in the windows of Big D's skyscrapers. Wishing she'd brought something to pin her shoulder-length hair off her neck, Rebel led the way through Base Ops. The vehicle Tank had advised would be waiting for them sat just outside the entrance.

"Nice." She eyed the midnight-blue Mustang convertible with approval. "The boy has taste. I'll drive, you navigate."

Ignoring the flash of annoyance in Blade's eyes, she slid behind the wheel. She was used to being in command—of a jet, a vehicle, her badass bike.

Once they were headed out of the lot, Blade called their contact. "My associate and I are in Dallas, Ms. Bauer."

He paused, the phone to his ear.

"That's right. We're with the government."

Another pause.

"It's a small agency. One I doubt you've heard of. But I can tell you the Department of Defense is interested in the information you posted about your grandfather."

Along with the Department of State, Rebel thought

wryly, the Department of Justice, and, oh, yeah, the White House.

"Why don't I give you my office phone number?" Blade was saying. "They'll verify my identity as well as that of my associate. Yes, it's open on the Fourth of July. We're a 24/7 operation."

Bauer obviously had second thoughts about two government agents knocking on her door, but Blade was gentling her like a spooked mare.

He was good at it, Rebel had to admit. Too good. The betting among OMEGA's female agents was that he owed his code name more to the swath he cut among the female of the species than his deadly skill with a knife.

And why not? The man was six-foot-two of lean, hard muscle. His lazy, come-hither grin and golden-brown eyes only added to the package. And to the list of reasons why Rebel kept her distance.

"Call the number I just gave you," he instructed their contact in a smooth, friendly tone that invited confidence. "Our Operations Center will verify we're on the level."

"What's the problem?" Rebel asked when he cut the connection.

"Hang on."

He thumbed a single key on his communications device. Like hers, it contained biometric and electronic scanners that could verify his identity with something close to the speed of light. Sure enough, it took him all of five seconds to reach Tank and warn him to expect a call.

"Our contact's turned skittish," he advised Rebel when he finished with Control.

"So I gathered. Why?"

"I don't know. She was cooperative enough when I talked to her earlier."

His phone pinged again a few minutes later. This time he put the call on speaker, and Rebel picked up instantly on the edge to Vivian Bauer's soft Texas twang.

"I, uh, talked to your office. They vouched for y'all."

"Good. So there's no problem?"

"No. Not really. It's just…" She gave a nervous laugh. "I got the strangest call a while ago."

"Strange how?"

"I couldn't really understand him. He spoke with a heavy accent."

"He was asking 'bout my grandfather, too," Bauer continued. "I never imagined my Facebook entry would generate so much interest. Oh, well…"

Obviously trying to shrug off her unease, she confirmed that she would wait for them at her grandfather's house.

She wasn't on the porch when they pulled up at the single-story, ranch-style home in one of Dallas's older neighborhoods. Nor did she answer the bell. Frowning, Blade tried the door and found it locked.

His glance cut to the late-model Nissan parked

behind the older Buick in the carport. "That's probably her car."

When he leaned on the bell a second, Rebel felt the hairs on the back of her neck stir again. Going with her gut, she fished a flat, pencil-thin rod out of her bag. Two twists, a click, and it was done.

"Well, what do you know?" She nudged the door with her toe. "It's open."

She heard him mutter something about illegal entry as she crossed the threshold—then stopped so abruptly he almost walked up her back.

With a smothered oath, she dropped to one knee beside the chunky brunette sprawled in a puddle of blood.

Chapter 2

Rebel found a pulse in the woman's neck, but the beat was as faint and fluttery as the wings of a dying bird. Most likely because of the bullet hole drilled through her throat.

"Call 911!"

The wound oozed hot, dark blood. Rebel slapped her palm against it while Blade whipped out his phone. His voice clipped and urgent, he relayed the situation, the address and his name and confirmed that he didn't know whether the shooter was still in the vicinity. All the while, Rebel kept pressure on the seeping hole.

"Hang on, Ms. Bauer," she pleaded. "Hang on. We're calling for medical assistance."

Blade tossed his phone at her. "Stay with her and keep the line open to 911. I'll conduct a search."

She groped one-handed for the instrument and saw him extract his Sig Sauer from its ankle holster. A bone throwing knife slid into his other hand. Palming it, he melted into the deepening shadows inside the house.

Frantically, Rebel searched her mind. Her Air Force survival training had included emergency first aid for some pretty drastic injuries. A bullet through the throat wasn't one of them. The fact that Vivian Bauer hadn't already bled out suggested the bullet had missed her jugular. Judging by the blood seeping through her fingers, though, Rebel guessed it had at least nicked the carotid.

She searched the dim interior for something to staunch the blood. She needed a towel, a jacket, anything. But the house had obviously been stripped of most of contents and scrubbed down after its owner had died. It was now mostly bare walls and unadorned furnishings.

Swearing, she yanked up the hem of her tank top and dragged it over her head. She had the stretchy fabric wadded and pressed against the hole when Vivian Bauer's lids fluttered up. Her eyes were blank for a second or two, then dazed, then, abruptly, flooded with terror. She jerked, trying to escape the pressure against her neck.

"Don't move, Ms. Bauer! We've called 911. The EMTs are on their way."

The woman's mouth opened. Her throat muscles worked. A bloody froth bubbled on her lips.

"Sssss…"

The sound tore at Rebel's gut. "Hang on, Vivian. Just a little longer."

"…ssscar."

Oh, Christ! She was trying to say something. Rebel leaned closer to bubbling red froth.

"Don't try to talk. Just hold on."

"Sssscar."

It was a whisper, a cry, a desperate plea.

"Okay. Okay. I got it. The person who shot you had a scar."

"Above…left…eye."

The last word came out on a sigh. Vivian Bauer's lids drifted down. A second later, her muscles went lax. Rebel knelt beside her, kept the wadded tank top pressed to the wound, but knew it was no use.

She was still on her knees when Blade returned. She angled her chin. Met his eyes. Shook her head. Biting out a curse, he holstered his weapon and reached down a hand. She wasn't too proud to take it. Not at that moment.

Somehow his arm ended up around her waist. A corner of her mind whispered that it felt good to lean against him for a moment. Then the wail of sirens had her pushing away.

His arm tightened, locking her against his side. "Hold still."

"I'm okay."

"Just hold it."

The sirens screamed closer. Strobes flashed like summer lightning in the windows. Brakes squealed outside.

Irritated now, Rebel elbowed his ribs. "Dammit, I'm all right. Let me go."

"Hell, woman, I know you're all right. I just thought you might want a cover-up."

She glanced to the side, saw his free hand working the buttons on his denim shirt. Belatedly, she realized the only thing between her and the first responders was the silly scrap of lace she'd opted for this morning instead of her usual sports bra.

"Oh."

"Yeah," he drawled, releasing her so he could work the last two buttons. "Oh."

When he tugged off the shirt and handed it to her, the sardonic glint that irritated the hell out of her was back in his eyes.

The Arlington police weren't real thrilled to learn a pair of government agents were on the loose within their jurisdiction, but Rebel and Blade managed to smooth their ruffled feathers. Particularly when they relayed information about the call Bauer had received and her last agonized whisper. That info and the hollow-point slug the Crime Scene Unit dug from the floor under the body provided the only clues to her killer's identity. CSU found no skin under her nails, no foot- or fingerprints, no tossed cigarette butt that might have provided a trace of saliva. Nor, apparently, had she been sexually molested or robbed. Her purse sat on the passenger seat of the Nissan, wallet and credit cards intact.

"So tell me again," the lead homicide detective said after the body had been removed from the scene and the house searched. "Why were you meeting with the vic?"

"She was going to show us an item of possible interest to the U.S. government."

He hiked a skeptical brow. "A chunk of Russian amber."

"Right."

"That she found among her grandfather's possessions."

"Correct."

His gaze cut to Rebel's blood-stained hands, then back to Blade. "Well, we didn't find any amber on the body or anywhere on the premises. So I guess we can assume whoever shot her had a possible interest in it, too."

"Guess so. You need us for anything else?"

He tapped the notebook where he'd recorded—and verified—the number for OMEGA control. "I know where to reach you if I do."

Neither Rebel nor Blade said much until they were headed back to the airport. She broke the tense silence first.

"We need to get Tank and Dodge working with

Interpol. They might have someone in the system who speaks English with a heavy accent and has a scar above his left eye."

"Several someones, I would guess." Blade already had his phone out. "I'll also have them do a trace on the call she received. And the hits on her Facebook site. Be interesting to see who visited the site besides the folks who left comments. Then, I think, we need to pay a visit to this NYU professor who floated the idea that the amber piece Bauer found in her grandfather's attic might be valuable."

Lightning concurred with their agenda when they briefed him late that night. He also advised them to take their passports with them to New York City.

"We've cleared you with the Russian government for a visit to St. Petersburg. Whatever Professor Dawson doesn't know about the Amber Room, the restorers working on-site at Catherine Palace will."

Rebel's pulse leaped. She'd visited St. Petersburg several times during her Moscow tour. He'd never made it out to Catherine Palace, though. The prospect of an up-close-and-personal tour of the fabled palace got her juices going.

The prospect of visiting it with Clint Black, she realized with some dismay, added to the kick. Her glance slid to where he conferred with Tank and Dodge Hamilton. She had to admit they were all prime specimens. Tank with his father's black hair, laser-blue eyes and the muscled shoulders of a Harvard sculler. Dodge with his rangy rodeo-rider's build that did wonders to a pair of jeans. Blade…

Hell! She had no business wondering if his sable dark hair was as soft and springy to the touch as it looked. Still less burying her nose in the collar of her borrowed shirt to sniff the faint leather-and-lime scent of his aftershave. She'd learned her lesson. She wasn't about get all goofy over a pair of whiskey-colored eyes and a killer grin.

Too bad Renee Dawson didn't share the same discriminating taste. The ash-blonde NYU professor started salivating the moment Blade introduced himself.

Rebel had to admit he'd triggered a similar Pavlovian response in her when he strode out to the taxi taking them to the airport this morning. The man looked hot as hell in jeans and a T-shirt. In slacks, an open-necked white shirt and a summer-weight sport coat he was sex on the hoof.

Rebel had dressed for travel, too, although the three-inch spike heels she'd paired with a slim black skirt, wide leather belt and cap-sleeved white blouse might not have been the best choice. The heels did put her almost at eye-level with Blade, however.

Not that the added height gave her any advantage with Professor Dawson. The fortysomething blonde had zeroed in on Blade like an unmanned Predator drone on a hot target.

"It's a pleasure to meet you, Mr. Black."

"Same here. And this is my partner, Victoria Talbot."

The professor gave Rebel a nod and pushed her glasses up on her forehead. The amethyst color of the frames matched her eyes, which remained locked on Blade.

"I had to rearrange my schedule a bit, but the dean said this meeting was important. He also indicated his call was from a very highly placed source."

Blade dodged the question behind that "very" and underscored the urgency of their visit with a blunt announcement. "The woman who posted a photo of what you suggested might be a medallion from the Amber Room was murdered last night."

"Oh, my God!" Shock leached the color from Dawson's cheeks. "Do you…? Do you think her murder is related to the medallion?"

"Since we didn't find it in her possession, that's a distinct possibility."

The professor struggled to recover. "What can I do to help?"

"Tell us what you know about the Amber Room and why you think Bauer's piece may have come for it."

"Yes. Yes, of course."

She dropped the jewel-framed glasses back onto her nose and skimmed the shelves lining her office before pouncing on a thick volume.

"This is the best reference on the subject. Sit here, Mr. Black." She gestured to the chair beside her desk. "Pull up that other chair, Ms.… Uh…"

"Talbot."

Rebel didn't roll her eyes. The gesture would have been wasted, since Dawson and Blade already had their heads together. She wanted to, though.

"As I'm sure you know," the professor began, "the semiprecious gem we call amber is the fossilized resin of giant conifer trees. These trees covered much of central and northern Europe some forty to sixty million years ago. When these trees sustained an injury of some kind—say a broken branch or an attack by beetles or perhaps a disease—they would 'weep' this resin. Over the millennia, the sap solidified and hardened into the substance we now call amber."

She flipped to a page that showed a variety of hues.

"Amber has been highly prized since prehistoric times. Most pieces range in color from yellow to orange to brown, although rare examples of green, red and blue have been found. The more valuable specimens are clear, almost translucent although many people prize specimens that include trapped insects or bits of organic material. Most experts agree the best amber comes from a huge deposit known as the Blue Earth, submerged beneath the Baltic Sea."

"The Blue Earth," Blade echoed. "I'm guessing that's the source of the Amber Room."

"Exactly."

She beamed as though he'd just solved the mystery of the Black Hole. Rebel tried not to gag.

"The history of that room goes back to the Teutonic Knights, a religious warrior sect that settled in what was then Prussia after the fall of Jerusalem in 1209. The knights took control of the lucrative amber trade and stockpiled huge quantities in their fortress monasteries to manipulate the market. They succeeded so well that amber at one time was worth twelve times more than gold."

"Monks, warriors and commodities speculators," Rebel observed. "All-around kind of guys."

She could have saved her breath for all the attention the other two paid her.

"After the knights were expelled from Prussia," Dawson continued, "Fredrick the First's court architect discovered tons of raw amber in the cellars of one of the knights' castles. He convinced the king to let him panel an entire room with the precious material, instead of just having it made into jewelry or decorative pieces."

She thumbed the pages and opened to a full-color, two-page spread of the most ornate chamber Rebel had ever seen, and she'd seen a few during her stopovers in Europe.

"The architect hired master craftsmen trained to work with amber. They used heat to soften it, then shaped it into pieces that they polished to a high shine with a mixture of cognac, honey and linseed oil."

Blade made a subtle movement. So subtle Rebel almost missed it. She shifted, trying to discern what prompted the move and spotted the hand now resting on his thigh. The professor didn't miss a beat in her lecture.

"The craftsmen backed the pieces with gold or silver leaf before gluing them onto wooden panels in intricate patterns. They then embellished the designs with diamonds, rubies and other precious gems. When they installed the panels in Charlottenburg Palace, the Amber Room was so dazzling that it became an instant, must-see attraction for aristocrats making a Grand Tour of Europe."

Right. And Blade's crotch appeared to have become a more modern-day attraction. Torn between amusement and annoyance, Rebel saw the professor's palm slide up an inch.

"So how did the room get from Prussia to Russia?" he asked calmly.

Either the man was made of stone, Rebel decided, or he was used to having women he'd known for all of twenty minutes feel him up. She went with option two.

"Peter the Great stopped in Prussia on his way to France in 1716. He was so taken with the Amber Room that Fredrick's son gave it to him to seal an alliance with the powerful czar."

Her fingers found the inseam of his jeans.

"The Czar had the panels shipped back to his capital of St. Petersburg," Dawson all but purred. "They went on display in several different palaces before Peter's daughter, Elizabeth, had them repaired and permanently installed at Catherine Palace—the czars' summer retreat on the North Sea."

Oh, for God's sake! Rebel appreciated art as much as the next gal but she didn't get all orgasmic over it. With a touch of impatience, she jumped forward several centuries.

"Where they remained until the Nazis invaded Russia in 1941."

Dawson looked less than pleased at having her learned discourse so rudely interrupted.

"Correct. By then they were deemed too fragile to take down and hide, so the curators of Catherine Palace constructed false walls to cover them. Unfortunately, the ruse didn't work. German soldiers quickly discovered the panels, dismantled them, packed them in crates and shipped them to Königsberg Castle in East Prussia."

The professor heaved a tragic sigh.

"The Allies bombed Königsberg in late 1944, as did the advancing Soviet Army in early 1945. Some believe the panels were lost when the Soviets pounded the castle into near rubble. Others theorize they were spirited away in the nick of time, since an eyewitness claims to have spotted twenty-six crates containing the amber panels being loaded aboard a train."

Rebel met Blade's quick glance. Another treasure train?

"Still another theory," Dawson continued, "is that the panels were loaded aboard the *Wilhelm Gustloff,* which was sunk by a Soviet submarine. And then there are the conspiracy theory proponents. They contend the Soviets inadvertently destroyed the panels when they blew up the Königsberg Castle ruins in 1966 but refuse to admit it, preferring instead to let the blame of the loss of this priceless treasure rest on German shoulders."

She sighed again and closed the book.

"Whatever the theory, the sad truth is one of the world's most exquisite works of art has never been found. Russian artisans have labored for the past fifty year to duplicate it. Their work is now on display in Catherine Palace. It's beautiful, but can't compete with the original."

"But pieces of the original room have surfaced," Blade prompted.

"Only two documented cases so far. One was a lacquer chest a Berlin woman reported owning after seeing a TV special on the Amber Room. It's believed to have been stolen separately, as it doesn't appear in German photos of Königsberg. Another was a mosaic believed to have been pilfered by a Nazi officer who accompanied the train to Königsberg. His heirs tried to sell the piece in 1997 for two and a half million dollars, but Art Loss Register detectives identified it as stolen and recovered it."

Interesting, Rebel thought. Apparently, light-fingered soldiers and officers in the armies of both sides had helped themselves to stolen property.

"What about this piece?" Blade laid a copy of Vivian

Bauer's Facebook photo in front of the professor. "Why do you think it came from the Amber Room?"

"I think it *might* have come from the Amber Room. The rose-petal motif looks very similar to one from a panel depicting the four seasons, but I don't have the exact dimensions of the original pieces. You would have to get those from the experts doing the restoration work."

"In St. Petersburg."

"In St. Petersburg."

Rebel blew out a breath. Good thing Lightning had advised them to bring their passports. Looked like they had a long flight ahead. She was mentally calculating their ETA in St. Petersburg when Blade eased his chair—and his thigh—away from the professor. Dawson made a moue of disappointment and pulled another book from her crowded shelves.

"This is the latest work devoted to the search for the missing panels. It's written by two investigative British reporters who unearthed actual documentation detailing the Amber Room's removal from St. Petersburg by the Nazis. You're welcome to borrow it."

Blade accepted the book with a smile that had the woman practically drooling. "Thanks."

"If there's anything else I can do for you, just call me."

"We will."

"Wait, let me give you my cell and home phone numbers."

She extracted an embossed card from the chrome holder on her desk and turned it over to scribble on the back.

"Call me," she reiterated. "Anytime."

Rebel tried to refrain from comment when they walked out into the noon heat. She honestly tried. She couldn't check the little huff of derision that slipped out, though.

"What?" Blade asked.

"Aw, c'mon. Don't act all innocent."

When he merely shrugged, she simpered and fluffed her hair. "Call me, big guy. Anytime. We can finish what I started in my office."

A rueful grin tugged at his lips. "You saw that, did you?"

"Hard to miss."

"The woman had information we wanted. I was just letting her deliver it her own way."

"Suuure you were."

His grin widened. "It's terrible the sacrifices we have to make for our country at times, isn't it?"

"Maybe I should have left you two alone," she retorted with a touch more acid than she'd intended. "Just imagine what you could have gotten out of her then."

He stopped in midstride, causing Rebel to do the same. Knapsack-laden students eddied around them. On the street just yards away, taxis chugged exhaust into the noon heat.

"If I didn't know better," he mused, that damned grin

still plastered across his face, "I'd say you were jealous."

"You're kidding, right?"

"Am I?"

"Oh, for—!"

Thoroughly disgusted, she spun on her heel. Or tried to. Her three-inch heel snagged on a crack, and Blade caught her as she teetered.

"Well, well," he taunted. "This is twice in as many days you've ended up in my arms. A few more times, and I'll think you're trying to tell me something."

Her first instinct was to deliver a swift knee to the gonads. Her more rational self acknowledged that might be a slight overreaction. Yet the taunt made something hot and heavy in her chest explode.

It was the elemental, timeless contest. Male versus female. Strength pitted against endurance. Only in this case, the combatants were two supremely confident, superbly conditioned individuals. And neither of them was used to backing down. Rebel came close, though, when she saw his gaze drop to her mouth and the grin fade.

He wasn't playing now. She told herself she'd be smarter to retreat and take up the battle another day, in another way. She had a second, maybe two, to signal a temporary truce before his hand slid up her arm and tunneled under the heat-dampened hair lying heavy on her nape.

When she didn't jerk away, he muttered something

that sounded suspiciously like, "What the hell." Then his mouth came down on hers, and the combustible mix of annoyance and reluctant attraction that had been building between them since Rebel's first day at OMEGA fireballed.

Chapter 3

Rebel had been kissed before. By her ex, of course, and a respectable number of males before and after. But she'd never experienced this dangerous duel of tongues and teeth and wills. Wild sensations shot straight to her belly, and when Blade shifted his stance and brought her hips against his, they rolled through the rest of her like a freight car.

An incredulous corner of her mind couldn't believe she was standing on the hot sidewalk outside NYU's Art History Building, a stone's throw from busy Washington Square, locking lips and hips. With Clint Black, for God's sake!

The rest of her mind, however, was close to overload. The taste of him. The scent of his aftershave. The movement of his shoulders under his sport coat. Rebel tried to process each separate sensation as it bombarded her but gave up after a few seconds. Or minutes. Or...

"'Scuse me, dude."

It took a bump and an amused apology from a student in waist-length blond dreadlocks to break her and Blade apart. Even then Rebel wasn't sure which of them pulled back first. That set off another set of alarms inside her still-reeling mind. Bad enough she'd let God's gift to womankind lay one on her. She'd stood there like an idiot, giving back as good as she got.

And it was good. Unbelievably good. Which rattled her even more. The only saving grace was that Blade looked almost as shell-shocked as she felt. A deep crease marked his brow as he offered an abrupt apology.

"Sorry."

"That makes two of us."

"I, uh, got a little carried away."

She was tempted to let him shoulder the entire blame. Unfortunately, she wasn't the type to take the coward's way out.

"We both did. It won't happen again."

The flat assertion erased his frown. In its place came a glint of something that looked dangerously close to a challenge.

"You sure about that, Talbot?"

She was. Especially now that she'd had a taste of the

kind of electricity the man could generate. She had more sense than to throw down another gauntlet, though.

"Look, let's not turn this into a contest. You know as well as I do how dangerous it is to get distracted during an op."

She could see he didn't appreciate the tart reminder. Probably because he'd racked up a lot more experience in the field than she had. Still, she drove the point home.

"One woman's dead already. I'm not looking to up the body count."

A now-familiar irritation flickered across his face. "I'm not, either. Or I wasn't," he added under his breath as he stepped to the curb to flag down a taxi.

His annoyed expression stayed in place when they climbed in and told the driver to take them to JFK. It was still there when he pulled out his communications device and keyed OMEGA Control.

"Tank, I need you to confirm those seats on the 5:20 p.m. flight to St. Petersburg."

No military jet this time. Rebel could have set one up given the priority of this mission, but their open-ended schedule once they hit Russia weighed against keeping an air force crew and aircraft standing idle for an indeterminate period.

"Yeah, we're finished at NYU." He speared a glance at the turbaned cab driver. "I'll call in an update when we get to the airport."

Tank took the update a half hour later. Dodge Hamilton was in the Control Center, his lanky frame ensconced behind a newspaper, but he was letting OMEGA's new recruit take the stick on this one.

From the various tales shared by his parents, sister and brother-in-law, Tank knew controller duty involved long stretches of mundane tasks spiked by moments or hours of heart-pumping action. So far, this op had provided both. Rebel's description of Vivian Bauer's last moments lingered in Tank's mind as he shared the results of the visit to NYU with Dodge, then called down to Lightning's executive assistant.

"I need to update the boss, if he's available."

"He is," Chelsea Jackson replied in the cool, cultured accent Tank couldn't quite place. It had a touch of Boston in it. So did his, for that matter, but it was a different Boston than the one he'd roamed during his years at Harvard.

"I'm on my way."

The titanium-shielded elevator whisked him noiselessly to the first floor. Already inoculated by security, he checked the screens to ensure no outside visitors had entered the building in the few seconds since his call, slapped his palm to the scanner and stepped into a reception area flooded with bright July sunshine. The light made a glowing nimbus of Chelsea's auburn hair and pretty well stopped Tank in his tracks.

This wasn't the first time he'd observed her at work. He'd stopped by the offices of the Special Envoy many times to visit Nick and met Chelsea Jackson soon after she was hired to fill the position once held by grandmotherly Elizabeth Wells.

They'd also socialized at several charitable functions sponsored by his parents. Tank had always found Chelsea intelligent and interesting to talk to, but he could understand why she'd gained a rep here at OMEGA for being distant. Among the male agents, anyway. She did her job with rapierlike efficiency and made it a point to keep her private life just that—private.

She also, Tank now realized with a small punch to the gut, had the achingly pure profile of a Renaissance madonna. When he said as much, however, something flickered in her brown eyes. It looked like amusement, but it came and went so swiftly he couldn't be sure.

"It's true," he insisted. "In this light, with your hair gleaming like dark copper, you could have stepped out of a painting by Raphael or Titian."

She dismissed the notion with a small shake of her head and stuck to business. "I informed Lightning that you were on the way down. Go right in."

She kneed a hidden button in the well of her ornate Louis XV desk to give him access to the inner sanctum.

"Thanks."

Chelsea returned his smile with a polite one of her own, but her gaze lingered on his broad shoulders as he made for the mahogany doors.

Adam Ridgeway II. Of the Boston Ridgeways, who could trace their family back to thirteenth-century England. Unlike Chelsea, who could trace hers only as far as the mother who'd raised her with a boozy blend of affection and indulgence. Her mom decamped with her latest lover two weeks before Chelsea's sixteenth birthday. After that, she'd fended for herself.

Renaissance madonna?

Ha! If only he knew.

Not that he would. She hadn't discussed her family, or lack thereof, with anyone at OMEGA. Except her boss, of course. Nick had reviewed her background data prior to approving her security clearance. He knew most of her secrets. And Chelsea had opened up a little with Victoria Talbot. The two women had started at OMEGA within weeks of each other. The way Rebel had dropped tough, macho Clint Black on his butt had won Chelsea's instant approval.

Except lately she'd sensed a shift in Rebel's attitude toward Blade and vice versa. They still yanked each other's chains. Still engaged in friendly competition during training sessions. But their professional relationship seemed to be edging closer to something more, well, volatile. Chelsea only hoped to heck it didn't blow up in their faces.

No, it wouldn't. Rebel had too much sense to let that happen, especially while she was in the field. Supremely confident in her friend's ability to maintain focus, she turned her attention to a stack of gilt-edged invitations awaiting an RSVP.

She would not fall into Clint Black's arms again, accidentally or otherwise. Rebel repeated that mantra more than once during the twelve-hour flight to St. Petersburg. The man was too cocky. Too pushy. Too sure of himself. And too much like her come-and-get-me ex.

It didn't help that he'd angled his seat back shortly after takeoff and zoned out. His long legs sprawled too close to Rebel's. Not even their spacious business-class seats could prevent an occasional knee or elbow bump.

Nor could she numb her senses with the alcohol that flowed so freely in business class. She didn't drink during an op unless circumstances dictated that she show she could hold her own. Instead, she downed too much coffee and spent the long flight reading the book Professor Dawson had pressed on Blade along with her card.

The professor hadn't exaggerated. The authors of *The Amber Room* had uncovered amazing documentation during their exhaustive research. These documents included transcriptions of German radio transmissions collected by Britain's formerly ultra-ultra-top secret Enigma project. One of these messages reiterated Hitler's exhortation to his troops to return the Amber Room to Prussia, where it belonged.

The documents also included excerpts from the diary of the Russian curator charged with stripping St. Petersburg's museums and palaces when the German's invaded. The curator and his army of helpers had worked day and night, so feverishly that the frantic packers got nosebleeds from bending over crates without letup.

The Germans had advanced to the suburbs of St. Petersburg when the crates were loaded onto a train and shipped eastward into Russia's vast interior. All except the Amber Room. That was deemed too fragile to move. Instead, the desperate curators had covered the panels with padding and constructed false walls to hide them.

The detailed account of the room's discovery by the Germans and subsequent removal to Königsberg Castle kept Rebel riveted right up to the announcement that they would be landing at Pulkovo Airport in twenty minutes.

Blade blinked instantly awake. Bringing up his seat back, he glanced at his watch. "Almost noon, St. Petersburg time. Hope Tank got that meeting with the folks at Catherine Palace set up for us."

"He did," Rebel confirmed. "I received a coded satellite transmission while you were sawing z's."

"You get any sleep?"

"No." She held up the book. "I've been reading."

He scraped a palm across his dark bristles. "You can brief me after I shave and clean up."

She vaguely recalled issuing a similar order when she'd hooked up with him at Andrews at the start of this op. She didn't care much for being on the receiving end, though.

"Yes, sir," she muttered to his back as he made for the galley and restrooms beyond. "Whatever you say, sir."

The heat wave gripping North America and Western Europe hadn't made it to this corner of the Baltic.

Although the summer sun wouldn't set until almost midnight, the daytime temperature hovered around sixty degrees. Just cool enough for Rebel to slip a hip-length leather jacket from her weekender to wear with her black skirt and somewhat wrinkled white blouse.

"There's Anton Gorsky."

She spotted the Russian contact whose photo and bio Tank had forwarded. The man was hard to miss. He stood almost six and a half feet tall and had shoulders like a bull moose. His bio listed his profession as a low-ranking official in Russia's Ministry of Culture. Rebel knew otherwise, but didn't betray their past association by so much as a flicker of an eyelid.

Blade had to suspect otherwise, too, when this supposedly minor bureaucrat supplied them with a signed and stamped visitors' permit that allowed them to bring their weapons into the country. He then escorted them past long lines of arrivals to a uniformed customs officer who peered suspiciously at their faces and ran their passports through a special scanner before waving them through.

When they emerged into thin, cool sunshine, Gorsky signaled the driver of a car idling at the curb. "I have been instructed to take you directly to Catherine Palace. You wish meet with the director, yes? Then the curator who oversees restoration of the Amber Room?"

"Right."

The driver popped the trunk so they could dump their bags and opened the vehicle's rear door for Blade and Rebel. Gorsky shoehorned himself into the front passenger seat.

"So," he commented, wedging his massive shoulders around, "you have visited St. Petersburg before?"

Blade shook his head, and Rebel gave him the answer he already knew. "I made a couple of trips while I was assigned to the U.S. Embassy in Moscow."

"Ah, then you know it is a city of glorious palaces constructed on a bend of the Neva River by Tsar Peter the first."

Some parts of it were glorious, she recalled all too vividly. Some were gritty and downright scary. She merely nodded, however, and commented that she hadn't made it out to Catherine Palace on either of her previous visits.

"Then I will tell you about it, yes?"

Gorsky launched into a description of the collection of summer palaces, parks and pavilions known as Tsarskoe Selo—the Tsar's Village—constructed by Peter the Great and his successors twelve miles south of the city. Since Rebel had read much of the area's history in the book borrowed from Professor Dawson's collection, she listened with half an ear while St. Petersburg's suburbs give way to a countryside dotted with small dachas. The well-tended gardens surrounding the dachas displayed the extraordinary abundance that came with upward of eighteen hours of sun a day.

Traffic was light so it took less than twenty minutes to reach the town renamed Pushkin in honor of one of

Russia's greatest poets, who'd studied at the school for boys established on the grounds of Catherine Palace. Broad avenues canopied by majestic elms led through the town.

"Look there," Gorsky said as they passed a set of tall gates flanked by military guards. "Behind those gates is Alexander Palace. The last tsar, Nicholas II, and his family were kept there under house arrest before they were exiled to Siberia. The Soviet military used the palace as a research institute until it was restored and reopened as a museum some years ago."

Rebel kept her face turned to the window. Gorsky was angled so that his was reflected in the glass. Their eyes met for the briefest instant before he resumed his patter. A few minutes later he directed their attention to a pair of massive wrought-iron gates.

"This is entrance to the palace built by Tsarina Elizabeth, daughter of Peter the Great. She named it Catherine Palace in honor of her mother."

They car swept past the gates and pulled into a parking lot jammed with tour buses. While Gorsky maneuvered his bulk out of the front seat, Rebel and Blade exited the rear. Their escort issued brief instructions to the driver in Russian before sweeping an arm toward a tree-lined walkway.

"We will approach the palace through the gardens."

Marble steps led to a succession of terraces decorated with statuary and fountains. Each garden was more elaborate than the last. All were crammed with tourists aiming digital and video cameras in every direction.

When they mounted a last set of steps and rounded a corner, Rebel fully expected something spectacular. What she got was incredible. She stopped dead, her jaw dropping as she took in what looked like a mile-long facade painted a vivid turquoise and lavishly adorned with white marble columns, pilasters and balconies, all embellished with bright, glittering gold leaf.

"It must have a thousand windows!"

"More," Gorsky asserted smugly.

The extraordinarily elaborate facade evoked images of other Baroque masterpieces Rebel had visited in her travels, but the five onion-shaped cupolas rising above what she guessed was the royal chapel gave Catherine Palace a uniquely Russian character. The cupolas, too, were beautifully, blindingly covered in gold leaf.

Gaping like any awestruck tourist, she couldn't help craning her neck as Gorsky escorted them to a marble staircase leading up to the center entrance.

"Have you ever seen anything like this?" she murmured to Blade.

"No."

The flat response brought her head around. "Don't let your enthusiasm carry you away."

He shrugged and turned his attention to the attendants on duty just inside the cavernous entrance. One of them handed each of the new arrivals a pair of blue plastic booties. Pointing to their feet, she nodded encouragingly.

"It is required," Gorsky apologized, "even though we have the special pass."

Once they were booted, he steered them around the magnificent marble staircase and down a long corridor lined on either side with doors showing aged wooden frames and wavy glass insets. Servants' quarters, Rebel guessed, now converted into offices, research cubicles, and storage areas.

"Here is the office of the director."

Gorsky reached for the knob, but Rebel spotted a welcome symbol two doors down. All the coffee she'd consumed on the plane was now demanding an outlet.

"Hang on a sec. I need to visit the ladies' room."

"I could use a quick stop, too," Blade added.

Gorsky shrugged. "Very well. I shall let the director know we are here, yes? Come in when you are done."

As she led the way down the hall, Rebel couldn't resist getting in a little dig.

"You hit the head before we landed, Black. You might want to have that weak bladder checked when we get home."

"Yeah, I might," he agreed, and promptly shoved her into the ladies' room.

"Hey!"

The two wooden stalls were empty. She saw that much in a brief flash before he slapped a palm against one of the stalls doors and crowded her against it. Then all she saw was the ice in his eyes.

"What's with you and this guy Gorsky?"

"What are you talking about?"

"Tell me, Talbot."

"I don't..."

"You've got five seconds."

She'd been scrambling for an answer, but that brought her chin up. "Or what?"

The ice turned lethal. "Or I extract the information."

"You and what army?"

The jeer was pure reflex and stupid as hell. She knew that even before he began a countdown.

"Four."

"You're starting to piss me off."

"Three."

"Dammit, Blade..."

"Two."

She didn't hear the whisper of bone on leather, barely saw him move. She felt the scalpel-sharp tip of his knife under her chin, though.

"One," he said softly, pressing the tip against her flesh.

Chapter 4

For a moment Blade thought sheer stubbornness would make the woman clamp her damned mouth shut. She was just bullheaded enough to force him to cut her. Whether or not he would have became a moot point when she gave a low hiss.

"He's one of ours."

"What?"

She couldn't turn her head with his blade pressed against the soft underside of her chin but she managed a swift, sideways glance at the door. When her furious gaze swung back, it lasered into him.

"Gorsky's one of ours," she ground out, her voice low and intense.

He didn't ease the pressure. "Why do you know this and I don't?"

"How I met him, when, has nothing to do with OMEGA."

The blade pricked her skin. A crimson drop welled at the tip.

"You want to try that one again?"

"I can't tell you, dammit! You're not cleared."

"And you are?"

"I was," she spit, "when I was assigned to the embassy in Moscow. Now back the hell off."

Blade ignored the snarled demand. He knew embassy personnel of every nation collected sensitive information on the countries they were assigned to. Military attachés, in particular, received special intelligence training. Some also engaged in covert activities.

Had Rebel?

He'd find out, Blade vowed. And fast. Easing away, he swiped the bone knife against his thigh.

"Better wipe the blood off your neck."

He left her peering into a mirror above the sink and cursing a blue streak.

As promised, the gorilla was waiting in the director's outer office. "I have told the director you are here," Gorsky pronounced. "As soon as Ms. Talbot returns… Ah, good. Here you are."

Rebel didn't look at Blade as she came in, her jacket zipped up to the throat. Nor did she betray any hint of the fury he knew had to be seething inside her. Was there fear churning around in there, too? Worry that she'd given away something she hadn't intended to?

He couldn't get that possibility out of his head. It hovered there while Catherine Palace's director greeted them in stilted but perfect English.

"Will you have tea?"

They accepted the polite invitation, and Vassily Mikailovitch himself filled glasses set in filigreed silver holders. Blade took his with milk, Rebel with lemon, Gorsky with three heaping spoons of sugar. When Mikailovitch had refilled his own glass, he gave them a look of polite inquiry.

"Perhaps you will explain your interest in our Amber Room?"

"We're looking into whether an amber rose medallion discovered a few days ago by an American woman might be from the original panels."

"Ah, yes. The Facebook entry."

"You saw it?"

Mikailovitch permitted himself a thin smile. "The Amber Room was Catherine Palace's great treasure. Many called it the eighth wonder of the world. Of course we watch closely for any reference to it in books or articles or on the internet."

And had been watching for more than sixty years, Blade guessed.

"The head of our Amber Room restoration team studied the Facebook photo," the director said. "While the piece is very well crafted, he does not believe it was part of the original room."

"Why?"

"We had only drawings, the memories of those who worked at Catherine Palace and one color photo taken in 1917 to use as reference when we recreated the room, you understand. But those sources tell us the hues in the Facebook rose are too dark and the curvature of the petals is wrong. We are attempting to contact the woman who posted this picture, however, to ask if our experts may examine the piece."

"She's dead," Blade informed him. "Murdered two nights ago."

"And the medallion?" he asked sharply.

"Missing."

Mikailovitch pinched his lips together. "How unfortunate."

Yeah, Blade thought. That was one way to describe cold-blooded murder.

"We would like to see the reconstructed room. Then talk to the head of the restoration team."

The director nodded and reached for the phone on his desk. "I will have a guide escort you to the room. Petr Kurov will meet you there."

Rebel didn't look at Blade while they waited for the guide. Her fury still simmered in a low, banked boil. She'd exerted an iron will to keep it from showing during the meeting with the director. Didn't give any sign of it now. She would make the man pay, though, and pay big for the bloodstain on her blouse collar.

Their guide was a dour matron in rubber-soled black Oxfords and a blue serge jacket stretched tight across her impressive chest. After receiving instructions from her boss, she led the visitors up the soaring central staircase to a roped-off passage that shuffled tourists through a series of interconnected salons.

As pissed as Rebel was, she forced herself to put aside thoughts of revenge and drink in the splendor of the salons. The portraits and silk hangings in the Blue Drawing Room were exquisite. The table in the Cavaliers' Dining Room was set with solid gold plate. Catherine the Great's crimson Throne Room evoked the extravagant magnificence of the court.

In each salon was a small black-and-white photo under glass. The photos showed the condition of the room after the Nazis withdrew. The damage was horrific. Collapsed roofs. Shattered windows. Blackened beams, gaping walls and rubbish piled everywhere. Rebel couldn't imagine how the Russians had restored Catherine Palace to such splendor in only six decades.

Or recreated an entire room crafted of rare and costly amber. She knew from her reading that the effort to create a full-scale replica had begun in the 1980s. Modern craftsmen moved into the same workshops their predecessors had used and relearned the fine art of working with amber. The new room was completed in 2003, just in time for the three hundredth anniversary

of St. Petersburg, and dedicated by President Putin in
a lavish ceremony attended by heads of state from all
around the world. But everything Rebel had read in no
way prepared her for the stunning reality of the recreated room.

"Whoa!"

She came to a dead stop just over the threshold, as
did the tourists around her. Blinking, she craned her
neck to take in the glowing ceiling, the ornate walls,
the candelabra, picture frames, heraldry and carved
reliefs all done in costly amber. It was a symphony, a
celebration, an achingly beautiful masterpiece ranging
in color from pale, lemony-yellow to smoky topaz.

"Come."

Their guide unclipped the velvet rope and hooked
an imperious finger at Rebel, Blade and Gorsky. When
others in the crowd tried to follow them off the pre-
scribed path, she stopped them with a scowl and curt
nyet.

Rebel tabled her still simmering anger at Blade and
moved slowly around the room. The intricate mosa-
ics and glorious colors dazzled. Overwhelmed. Amber
inlaid with wood and glittering gilt decorated the walls,
the ceilings, the furnishings, even a magnificent eight-
foot-tall grandfather clock. Trying to take it all in, she
moved to the panels depicting the four seasons. Fall she
identified by its harvest motif. Moving past winter, she
stopped at spring.

Medallions in dozens of different shades and shapes

were used to create the spring blossoms. Rebel bit her lip and scoured the flower bouquets.

"Here it is."

She'd been so absorbed in her hunt that Blade's low murmur made her start. Then again, it could have been the warm wash of his breath on her cheek as he leaned closer to examine the bouquet of roses.

When Rebel jerked away, the quick glance he shot her said she had good reason to be so jumpy. Obviously, her terse revelation in the ladies' room hadn't answered the questions in his mind.

Tough. That's all he was going to get out of her. She, on the other hand, would exact a yet-to-be-decided penalty for...

"Ya Kurov."

The quiet announcement cut through Rebel's seething thoughts. Tamping down her anger once again, she turned to the white-coated, white-haired scarecrow who'd entered through a side door hidden among the intricate carving.

"He is Kurov," Gorsky translated.

The head of the Amber Room restoration team was thin to the point of emaciation. Bony wrists protruded from the cuffs of his coat. His cheeks formed sunken caverns. But when he spoke of the Facebook photo, his eyes blazed with the passion of a man who'd dedicated his entire professional life to a single room. Extracting a copy of the photo from his coat pocket, he positioned it alongside the recreated panel. A gnarled finger jabbed from one bloom to the other.

"As you can see," Gorsky interpreted, "the rose in the photo is darker in color."

"That could be due to camera settings," Rebel pointed out.

When Gorsky relayed her comment, Kurov bobbed his head but had her count from the tight center bud of one amber rose to its unfolded outer petals. The bloom in the photo had fewer petals, and those it did have appeared rougher at the edges.

"But the workmanship is very fine," Gorsky translated. "Very fine, indeed. Kurov says…"

He broke off, frowning, and fired several questions at the restorer. The answers made him purse his lips.

"Kurov says he told the men who came yesterday the same thing."

"What men?"

The curator glanced at the guide standing a few feet away.

"Did one of them have a scar above his eye?" Rebel persisted.

The question seemed to shrivel the man inside his white coat. He dodged the question and said only that he very much wished to examine the piece in the photo.

The news that the woman who'd posted it was murdered and her amber medallion had disappeared shook him a good deal more than it had his boss. Kurov took a step back, his eyes shocked, and poured out a spate of Russian.

"He says he must go. He has much work to do."

"Wait."

"No, no, he cannot."

The restorer turned away, hesitated, and appeared to remember his manners. He turned back and offered a gnarled hand to Blade.

"Kurov wishes you good health..."

He faced Rebel. His skin felt dry and paper-thin against hers.

"...and he thanks you for your interest in the Amber Room," Gorsky intoned.

The whisper was so low she would have missed it if she hadn't read it on Kurov's lips.

A street, a number, a time.

She didn't blink, didn't alter her politely disappointed expression by so much as a muscle twitch. "Please thank him for us, too," she instructed.

"So," Gorsky pronounced when he'd summoned their driver and squeezed into the front seat again. "You wish to go to the hotel and rest, yes? Then I will take you to my favorite restaurant. We have a little vodka, a little borscht and the finest *pirozhki* in all of St. Petersburg."

The mere thought of savory, deep fried dumplings stuffed with onions, mushrooms and ground beef made Rebel's stomach leap for joy. If not for Kurov's whisper and the cool watchfulness in Blade's eyes, she would have taken Gorsky up on his offer instantly.

"Sorry," she said with real regret. "I have to pass. I didn't sleep on the plane. I'm starting to feel it."

"But you must eat."

"I'll get something at the hotel."

"So it will be just us men, then." Gorsky slewed his massive shoulders around to face Blade. "I know another place," he said with a wink. "Good vodka, good borscht, and the best... How do you say? The best endowed waitresses in all St. Petersburg."

"Hooters on the Neva. Sounds like my kind of place."

"Surprise, surprise," Rebel drawled.

"But I'll take a pass, too," he finished, his hawk's eyes on her.

"How cruel you are." Gorsky heaved an exaggerated sigh. "You leave me no choice but to go home to my wife."

Their hotel was a modern tower of concrete and glass that catered primarily to business execs and foreign officials. Blade assumed as a matter of course the rooms were bugged. The KGB might have gone out of business in 1991, but its successor, the FSB, was alive and well.

He and Rebel were silent in the elevator taking them to the third floor and didn't speak until they were at the doors of their adjoining rooms.

"You've got five minutes," he told her.

"Then?"

"Then we walk."

And talk, he vowed grimly when she shut her door

in his face. Keying his own room, he dropped his carryall on the bed before flicking open the heavy drapes. The windows gave a sweeping view of the Neva River spanned by its elaborately decorated bridges. Across the river, the green-and-white facade of the Winter Palace took up almost an entire block. Flanking it were the mansions and palaces Peter the Great's courtiers had built when the tsar moved his royal court from Moscow to his new city on the Neva.

Blade studied the view for another moment or two before sliding his phone from his pocket. He couldn't risk a voice transmission given the probability of bugs, but Lightning's wife, Mac, had built so many levels of encryption into the phone that he had no qualms about sending a coded text. Still, his thumbs hovered over the keys for several moments more before tapping out a message.

Urgent—need info on covert ops Rebel
engaged in while Asst Air Attache in Moscow

He hesitated, feeling something wrench inside him, then added a critical caveat: if any.

Jaw tight, he snapped the phone shut. This was the first time, the only time, in all his years with OMEGA that he'd harbored so much as a shred of doubt about one of his fellow operatives. The fact that it was Rebel who'd spawned the question had acid churning in his stomach. He couldn't ignore the silent signal he'd intercepted, though. One brief flicker, one shared glance between her and Gorsky. If Blade had been looking out the window, he would have missed it.

He jammed the phone into his pocket, his mind shouting denials. Victoria Talbot had graduated from the Air Force Academy, for God's sake! Spent more than a decade in uniform before Lightning recruited her. She and Blade had worked several ops together, and she'd always given two hundred percent to the mission.

Okay, the woman's ripe mouth and long legs had triggered more than one erotic fantasy inside his head. And yes, he had yet to erase the lingering memory of her body ensnared with his during that idiotic kiss on the sidewalk outside NYU. He wasn't making excuses for himself or her. Wasn't questioning his own instincts. But…

Christ! Who the hell was he kidding? Everything in him wanted OMEGA Control to come back with incontrovertible evidence that Victoria Talbot was exactly who she claimed to be.

Striding to the bathroom, he wrenched the faucets with barely controlled savagery and doused his face with ice-cold water. Three minutes later, he rapped on her door.

She'd used the brief interval to change into jeans, a short-sleeved tank with a mock turtleneck and a pair of silver spangled ballet flats more comfortable for walking. Blade chose a small, crowded restaurant some three blocks from their hotel. It sat well down a side street, away from the tourist traffic. The heavy scent of fried potatoes and sausage permeated the clouds of cigarette smoke rising from scarred wooden tables and booths. The glass shelves behind the bar displayed an astonishing variety of vodkas and local beers. The menu was chalked on a green slate hung next to the bar.

The patrons hunched over their drinks wore mostly jeans, with a scattering of leather. Rebel might have fit right in if not for her height, her hip-swinging stride and her air of cool self-confidence as she wove through the tables. Heads turned, glances sharpened, and more than one male tracked her progress to a booth.

The waitress who came to take their order raked her with a keen eye, too, before turning to Blade. Her cheeks creased in a smile. He returned it and shook his head in response to her query.

"Ah!" She switched to thick, guttural English. "I bring you Western menu."

Blade glanced from the waitress to the woman seated across from him. "Why don't you order for us?"

Rebel's eyes locked with his. Then her mouth took a sardonic twist and she reeled off a spate of Russian. The waitress nodded and went back to the bar.

A taut stillness encased the booth, shutting out the chink of bottles and the other patrons' conversations. Rebel was the first to break it.

"I took Russian at the Air Force Academy, which is one of the reasons I was selected for the attaché job. The air force also sent me to the Defense Language

Institute at Monterey for a brush-up before I left for the assignment in Moscow. As I'm sure you'll ask Tank to verify," she taunted, "if you haven't already."

Blade wasn't buying it. She'd had plenty of opportunity to display this particular language skill during the dangerous op they'd worked just months ago involving Dodge Hamilton and the icily beautiful Russian missile officer he'd subsequently married.

"You never spoke to Larissa Petrovna in her own language," he countered slowly. "Not in my hearing, anyway."

The unspoken implication in that last phrase sparked a hot retort.

"I didn't speak to Lara in Russian because she *is* Russian. If you'd ever pulled attaché duty, you would know we're trained to listen and observe, not showboat our linguistic ability to the other side."

She sat back, blew out a breath and made an obvious effort to rein in her temper.

"Look, I like Lara. If I'd needed to communicate with her in her own language while we were tracking the bastard who'd kidnapped and tried to kill her, I would have. In a heartbeat! But I didn't."

He wanted to accept her tart explanation. Wanted to be convinced. Blade couldn't believe how much. He said nothing, however, while the waitress approached. Smiling, the woman deposited a cloudy glass and a cup of thick, sludgy coffee on the table.

"Is best vodka," she informed Blade, nudging the glass in his direction. "From Samara."

"Thanks."

"Pozhaluystra."

When she sauntered away, he looked over to find Rebel shaking her head.

"Do you even know you do that?" she asked acidly.

"Do what?"

"Advertise your availability to every female who might be even remotely interested."

Frowning, he cupped the glass. He would be the first to admit he wasn't the most sensitive guy in the world when it came to social nuances. Still, he was pretty sure he hadn't been coming on to the waitress. Irked, he turned the question back on the questioner.

"Is this a subtle attempt to change the subject, Talbot, or are you trying to tell me you might be interested?"

"No, and God, no! For the record, though, I didn't order the vodka. That was a gift from your friend at the bar. I would take it in small doses if I were you."

He did, but even a cautious swallow ripped down his throat. "Good Lord!"

Smirking, she waited for the explosion in his belly to subside before picking up where she'd left off. "And the reason I didn't order vodka is that we have an appointment later."

"With?" he got out on a hoarse croak.

"Petr Kurov. One a.m. At number seventeen Nevsky Prospect."

Ignoring the aftershocks in his gut, Blade narrowed his eyes. "Did Gorsky set this up?"

"No, Kurov did, when he whispered to me at Catherine Palace."

He swallowed that with a nasty dose of suspicion. "Why 1:00 a.m?"

"I'm guessing because the sun won't set until close to midnight and he doesn't want his friends and neighbors seeing him meet with two Americans." Her smile was a cool, mocking challenge. "Now you just have to decide whether you believe me."

Chapter 5

Tank skimmed the message on the screen for the second time.

It was early evening St. Petersburg's time, mid-morning in D.C. He'd been at the Control Center all night but had grabbed a quick shower, a shave, and breakfast around 8:00 a.m. Dodge had waited for him to come back recharged before zipping home to do the same himself. He was only a phone call away and could return to the Control Center within minutes if necessary.

Lightning wasn't on-site, either. He'd flown to New York for a meeting with some UN delegates who couldn't be rescheduled. That left Tank, two communications techs, an intelligence analyst and the frizzy haired genius who headed OMEGA's Field Dress unit within shouting distance of each other.

He was tempted to give one of them a yell. The request on the screen was labeled "urgent." Blade wanted info on any covert ops Rebel might have engaged in while assigned to Moscow as an assistant air attaché, like now.

Tank had served in the military as a JAG. Despite the TV show of the same name, most Marine Corps legal types didn't get up close and personal with covert ops or international intrigue. He knew, however, that military attachés were trained to observe and collect sensitive information. Obviously, Blade thought Rebel may have done just that.

So why didn't he ask her for verification? Why send an urgent back-channel request?

Tank might be OMEGA's newest recruit, but he'd spent his entire life in the agency's shadow. He didn't need to be told that an operative's first rule of survival in the field was to trust his or her instincts. For some reason, Blade's instincts were telling him he needed more information about his partner on this op.

Dragging his gaze from the screen, Tank scribbled a name and office symbol and walked over to one of the comm techs.

"Can you can get this guy on a secure line for me, Jane?"

"That's what we do." The cheerful mother of three

glanced at the note. "Robert DeLeon, Senior Analyst, Defense Intelligence Agency, coming right up."

Having so many Washington connections helped. As did having a knock-out for a sister. Bob DeLeon had dated Samantha while she was in med school. They'd gone their separate ways since then, but the former Princeton hoop star hadn't given up hope of resuming relations. A fact he reiterated when he came on the line.

"Hey, Tank. How's that gorgeous sister of yours?"

"Busy treating earthquake survivors in Mali right now."

"Damn! Tell her I need treating when she gets home."

"You're beyond hope of any cure, DeLeon."

"That's what Samantha said," he admitted. "Several times. So what can I do for you?"

"You can tell me who to talk to about a former air force officer's covert activities while serving as an assistant air attaché in Moscow."

DeLeon didn't reply for several seconds. When he did, he was obviously choosing his words with care. "I see you called in on a secure line. I've pinpointed your location, but I'll need a flash code before I act on your request for information."

"Hang on." Tank glanced across his console to Jane O'Conner. "He needs a flash code."

Nodding, she hit two keys. "He's got it."

Tank hadn't earned his nickname by backing away from a challenge. It took several calls and some dogged persistence, but he finally penetrated the maze of secrecy surrounding the world of covert intelligence collection. Propping back his chair, he studied the notes he'd made to himself over the course of several conversations.

Who knew Rebel was fluent in Russian? Or that she'd trained as a spook after several years in the cockpit? Lightning, obviously, since he'd specifically chosen her for this op. Interesting. He thumped his chair down and had started to draft a response to Blade's message when another thought hit him.

Tank's mother was a linguist. Had written several books on universal phonetics, in fact. She always claimed people with an ear for the nuances of speech made the best spies. His older sister had that same ear. Gillian picked up a working knowledge of Mandarin during her State Department assignment to Beijing. The facility had proved invaluable when Jilly jumped feetfirst into an OMEGA op in Hong Kong. As she frequently pointed out, like mother, like daughter.

So maybe…

It was just a hunch. A way-out-there thought. But it got Tank digging further into the background of a WWII infantry grunt with the German-sounding name of Thomas Bauer, the late grandfather of the late Vivian Bauer.

His first hit came from a check of census data and immigration records. The second, after another round of calls to the archives of what was then the U.S. Army's Office of Special Operations. Absorbed in the notes he was furiously compiling, he didn't notice Dodge had returned until the operative dropped into the seat beside him.

"You look pretty intent," the lanky Wyoming native commented. "What's happening?"

"A couple of things. First, Blade wanted to know if Rebel did any spook work during her air force days."

"Did she?"

"She did."

Dodge took a moment to absorb that. "Guess that doesn't surprise me. She sure transitioned from the military to OMEGA smoothly. What else have you got?"

"I rooted around a little more into Thomas Bauer's background. Turns out his parents emigrated to the States from Germany in 1926. When the U.S. entered WWII, the Office of Special Operations searched for German-speaking recruits and found out Bauer spoke it at home while growing up. The OSS yanked him from his infantry unit, trained him as a saboteur and dropped him behind enemy lines in the last years of the war."

He paused for effect, his eyes glinting.

"Bauer's target was the East Prussian stronghold where his parents, his grandparents and several generations of Bauers before them lived."

Dodge got it in one. "Königsberg?"

"Königsberg. The last known repository of the Amber Room."

"So that's where Bauer picked up his souvenir!"

"That would be my guess."

His brow knit, Dodge mentally reviewed their growing dossier of information on the missing treasure. "Didn't the Soviets sift through every ounce of rubble in Königsberg after the war, searching for the panels?"

"They did. Several times. Which is why most experts believe they were destroyed in the allied bombing raids. But…"

Smug satisfaction colored Tank's voice.

"According to his immigration application, Thomas Bauer's father dug sewers for a living before coming to the States. Stands to reason a sanitation worker would know every tunnel, every underground passageway in the city. Also stands to reason a son about to be sent into Königsberg as a saboteur would pump his father for that information."

"Damn, Ridgeway! You've been busy."

"That's not all. I found out one of Bauer's cousins is still alive. I'm thinking Blade or Rebel may want to pay her a visit."

Blade stood by the window still streaming light at 11:00 p.m., the phone to his ear. The voice signals sent from OMEGA were scrambled and couldn't be picked up by any listening devices that might be planted in the room. His careful replies could, however. So all he did was thank his unnamed caller for the update and snap his phone shut.

He pulled in a long breath, feeling as though he'd just bounced off the five-ton elephant that had been tap-dancing on his chest. Rebel's story checked out. Tank hadn't dug up all the details. Those remained buried in top secret DIA and CIA files. But he did confirm that Major Victoria Talbot had worked with an unnamed St. Petersburg source to gather information on a highly classified military research project. The Russians had subsequently put the project on the back burner for lack of funding. The U.S. was pressing ahead with it.

Blade could axe his insidious doubts. Trust his partner on this op. Breathing easy for the first time in more than eight hours, he crossed to the connecting door between their rooms.

They'd left it open by mutual consent. Or mutual suspicion. Whatever the reason, they'd filled the hours until their meeting with Kurov with desultory conversation and reading.

He wasn't sure when Rebel had dozed off. Sometime around nine-thirty or ten, he thought. He was surprised she'd lasted until then, considering she'd spent the entire flight to St. Petersburg pouring through Professor Dawson's book. It was in her lap now, propped up by nerveless hands.

He stopped just over the threshold and studied the sleeping woman. She was curled into a loose ball in her room's overstuffed armchair. A silky tangle of hair brushed one shoulder. Her lashes fanned her cheeks. Her breath snuffled in, sighed out.

Blade's mouth twisted. He might as well admit it. Tank's call had relieved more than his mind. It had churned up his contradictory feelings for Talbot and distilled them down to one inescapable essential. He wanted this woman with an ache that damned near doubled him over whenever he let it slip past his guard.

Like now. It was there, knifing into his belly when he lifted her out of the chair and into his arms.

"Nnnngh."

She gave an inarticulate grunt and blinked up at him owlishly.

"Whatimeizit?"

"Almost eleven. You can sleep another hour."

Her head flopped against his shoulder. Her arm looped around his neck. With another grunt, she burrowed her nose in the side of his throat.

He tried to ignore the firm, full breast mashed against his chest and carried her to the bed. When he bent to stretch her out on the brocade cover, however, she wouldn't stretch.

"C'mon, kid. You might as well get comfortable."

Her arm remained hooked around his neck. He shifted until he sat on the mattress, her bottom resting on his thighs, and saw the question in her brown eyes.

"I was half-asleep..."

"You were all the way asleep."

"...but I think I heard you talking to someone."

"I got a call from home."

Home being their agreed on code for OMEGA. She blinked more fully awake.

"And?"

"And they confirmed delivery of the items we discussed at dinner tonight."

"They did, huh?" Her mouth curved into the irritating smirk he disliked so much. "Satisfied, Black?"

"Almost."

One dark blond eyebrow arched. "So what's it going to take to get you all the way there?"

He couldn't help himself. She looked so smug, so self-possessed.

"We don't have the time it would take for either of us to satisfy the other."

Rebel sucked in a breath and wondered for a wild moment if she was misreading the glint in his golden-brown eyes. Nope, no mistake. That was a taunt. A dare that stirred two instant reactions.

One, she knew better than to rise to such an obvious challenge. Two, she wanted him to knock it right back down his throat.

There was a third desire muddled up in there somewhere. One that made the muscles low in her belly quiver and warned her she was playing with fire when she reached up and undid the top button on his shirt.

"Correct me if I'm wrong," she murmured, "but I seem to recall someone saying I could snooze for another hour."

She popped the second button and had the fierce satisfaction of hearing Blade suck air this time.

"I don't know about you," she purred, trailing a nail

over the expanse of tanned chest she'd exposed, "but an hour might just do it for me."

She bent forward and nipped the smooth, taut swell of muscle. Harder than she'd intended, apparently, because he had her flat on her back less than two seconds later. He leaned over her, caging her in, igniting a need that burned like phosphorous. He had to have read the white-hot hunger he'd stirred, but he gave her an out.

"You sure you want this?"

Hell, no! The denial fog-horned through her mind, forcing her to catalogue all the things that irritated her about this man. He was too cocky. Too overbearing. Too damned magnetic to the female half of the world's population.

More to the point, she had to consider their mission. She'd already used it as a safety valve during that idiotic moment on the street outside NYU's art history building. She fully intended to use it again. And would have, if the memory of how his mouth had molded hers back there in New York hadn't slammed into her.

"Yes," she breathed. "I want it."

Him, she corrected. She wanted him. Had wanted him since the day she'd dropped him on his ass. She could admit it now, with his hands and mouth demanding a response from hers.

She gave it. Eagerly. Greedily. Her head angled. Her hips shifted. Breathing hard and fast now, she wedged her hands between their straining bodies and fought the remaining buttons of his shirt. Two gave, but the last held on stubbornly until Rebel tore it loose.

He was just as impatient. Hands rough, he yanked off the mock turtleneck she'd put on in place of the blouse with the bloodstained collar. She fell back on the now twisted bedcovers and reached for him.

He froze, his chest six inches from hers, his gaze locked on the small round Band-Aid she'd stuck on after washing the nick. An equal mix of regret and exasperation roughened his voice.

"Don't push me like that again."

She huffed indignantly. "Is that supposed to be an apology?"

He buried his fists in her hair. "Dammit, woman, don't you know how close you came to the edge?"

"No," she shot back. "Tell me."

When he didn't answer, her eyes searched his. What she saw in them sent a ripple down her spine. Not a shiver exactly. But close. Too close.

"Would you have cut me?" she asked in a husky whisper. "Really cut me."

"Yes."

He hadn't hesitated. Hadn't made any attempt to sugarcoat his curt reply. That answered one question in Rebel's mind. Clint Black would take whatever measures he deemed necessary to accomplish their mission. The knowledge satisfied her on a professional level, and stirred a whole host of questions on another, not least among them was whether she would go to the same extreme. The fact that she didn't know distracted her so much she almost missed the tick in the side of his jaw.

She didn't miss the way his fists tightened in her hair, though. Or the sudden savagery in the mouth that covered hers. He'd been forced to cut someone before, she understood with blinding certainty. Someone he'd trusted. The realization burned a hole in her heart. It also made her lock her arms around his neck and strain against him. Their tongues met in mounting urgency, and he had her naked almost before she knew it was happening.

The man was good at this, she acknowledged ruefully. Way too good. Then she wiped the thought from her mind and gave herself up to the wild sensations he generated with his teeth and his tongue and his busy, busy hands.

He'd worked his way down to her breasts when a faint glimmer of sanity surfaced.

"Clint…"

His teeth rasped her distended nipple.

"Clint!" Gasping, she arched her back. "We agreed. Back in New York. This isn't smart."

"Right." He slid his body over hers, moved up to her mouth. "We did."

"We. Should. Stop."

"Right again."

"You first."

Laughter rumbled in the chest crushing her into the

mattress. The sound drove out her last remnant of sanity and made her desperate for more. Throwing herself to one side, she used the momentum to roll him onto his back. Her hands were frantic at the waistband of his jeans when the phone on the desk across the room shrilled.

"Dammit all to hell!" She threw a frustrated glance at the phone and scowled when it shrilled again. "Don't move," she ordered.

"No, ma'am."

Snatching up his shirt, she dragged it on and stomped across the room.

Blade crossed his hands under his head and enjoyed the view. Her hair was a tangled, tawny mess. Her bare legs seemed to stretch forever below his shirttail. And damned if he didn't spot a dimple in her left cheek when she leaned across the desk to snatch up the receiver.

"Yes?"

He watched her, fully aware that the relief generated by the call from OMEGA Control had battered at his restraint. It had collapsed completely when she'd curled in his arms and…

"On, no!"

Slowly, Blade brought down his arms.

"Thank you for letting us know." She hung up and turned. "That was Anton Gorsky, our escort from the Ministry of Culture."

The use of the man's title was deliberate. Another signal, this one for any possible listening devices.

"Anton just heard on the eleven o'clock news that Petr Kurov, the curator we spoke with at Catherine Palace this afternoon, had a tragic accident."

"What happened?"

"Apparently…" She wet her lips. "Apparently, he's had some balance problems. Anton says his neighbors reported that he'd fallen several times recently. This time he stumbled and went right through the window of his fifth-floor apartment."

Stumbled, hell. His mind racing, Blade swung off the bed. What had Kurov known? And who were the men he'd mentioned at Catherine Palace? The curator had turned five shades of pale when Rebel asked if one of them had a scar above his eye.

Had Vivian Bauer's killers tracked Kurov to his apartment? Beat or choked a key piece of information about the Amber Room out of him? Pushed him out a window? If so, that was twice now scarface and pal had left a corpse in their wake.

Vowing it would be the last, Blade crossed the room. He slid his hand through the heavy silk of her hair and cupped her nape.

"I would suggest we pick up where we left off, but…" He squeezed her neck. "Takes the edge off, doesn't it?"

She got the message. Following his lead, she let out a long sigh. "It does."

"I need some coffee. Get dressed, and we'll go out."

The streetlights came on just as they emerged from the hotel. In the last, hazy glow of St. Petersburg's white night, Blade hooked his arm through Rebel's and briefed her on the second part of Tank's call.

Nobly, she refrained from pointing out the parallel between Sergeant Thomas Bauer's work with the OSS and her own covert activities, but the fact that his father had dug sewers for a living evoked a gasp.

"The authors of the book the professor lent us cited several references suggesting the Nazis moved the Amber Room panels out of Königsberg Castle into an underground bunker for safekeeping. The Soviets searched for decades after the war but couldn't find it."

"Maybe Bauer had better luck."

"Maybe."

When she whipped out her phone, Blade glanced down at her. "What are you doing?"

"Getting us on the next flight to Königsberg. Which, by the way, the Soviets renamed Kaliningrad."

Chapter 6

While Rebel used her phone to check transportation to Kaliningrad, Blade used his to tap into the State Department database and call up information on the city and the country that shared the same name. A State Department map showed Kaliningrad to be a tiny slice of territory separated from Mother Russia by more than five hundred miles. The Russian satellite state sat wedged between Poland and Lithuania and boasted a small coastline on the Baltic Sea.

Allied and Soviet bombing raids had pulverized Kaliningrad—then Königsberg—in the closing months of WWII. After the war, the Soviets annexed the former East Prussian province and made it the headquarters of their Baltic Fleet. Since it was the only Russian Baltic port to remain ice-free all year round, Moscow had stubbornly hung on to it after the Soviet Union fell apart.

Kaliningrad's physical separation from Russia had some unintended side effects, Blade gathered from the State Department brief. The distance weakened the central government's authority in its satellite state. So much so that some DOS wag had likened Kaliningrad to the lawless frontier of America's Old West. Except their cowboys ran guns, drugs and white slaves instead of cattle.

"The fastest way to get there is by air," Rebel announced. "We can… Crap!"

"What?"

"The only direct flight is aboard a Belorussian variant of the DC-6."

"I jumped out of a DC-6 down in South American during my Army special ops days," Blade mused. "As I recall, it was a bucket of rust held together by wire and spit."

"I'm not surprised. The last DC-6 rolled off the assembly line in 1958. It is—or was—a great airframe, but there's no way I'm climbing into the back end of one."

"We could have Tank set up a car."

He was envisioning a sporty, kilometer-eating convertible and a night spent along the way when she nixed the idea.

"We would have to drive through Latvia and

Lithuania, and we don't have visas. We could get them, but border crossings from Russia take forever since the Baltic States thumbed their noses at their former Soviet masters and joined NATO. Let me check the train schedules."

When she tilted her phone to catch the glow from the streetlamps, the light illuminated her face. Her mouth was devoid of lip gloss and slightly swollen, Blade noted with a tug low in his belly. He could still taste her, and felt an instant craving for another sample.

"We're in luck," she announced. "A fast train departs the South Station at 5:50 a.m. Since all Russian trains run on Moscow time, we're actually talking four-fifty." She thumbed the phone keys. "I'll reserve our tickets online but we'll need to pick them up at the station at least sixty minutes before departure."

Blade checked his watch. That still gave them a couple hours. Enough time to finish what they'd started before Gorsky's call. Or not.

Rebel hadn't slept at all on the flight over and had only napped for an hour or so tonight. She had to be running on fumes. What he wanted to do with her would drain the rest. Not a real smart move on his part, especially if someone had in fact sent Kurov sailing through a window. The bodies were starting to stack up.

"Besides," he told her in the elevator taking them up to their rooms, "the next time I get you naked, I damned well don't intend to keep one eye on the clock."

She slanted him a quick glance. "You that sure of yourself?"

"Yeah," he responded with a grin. "I am."

Wrong answer. He realized that as soon as he saw the chill descend.

"God forbid I should spoil your perfect record," she muttered.

The elevator door pinged open. He followed her into the hall, frowning. "I'm not keeping score here, Talbot."

"Good to know."

Her acerbic tone implied exactly the opposite. She keyed her room and when he entered after her, she gestured to the still open connecting door.

"Close that behind you, will you? I'm going to take a quick shower and pack. I'll buzz when I'm ready to go."

"Hold on a minute. You need to explain what just happened."

"You said it yourself. Too many bodies stacking up. Let's just leave it there."

"The hell we will."

Her temper flashed, melting the ice in her eyes, but she battled it into submission. "We have to pack, check out and catch a train. How about we table further discussion until we're aboard?"

Even after they'd stashed their bags in the overhead rack and claimed facing seats in the first-class compartment, Rebel was in no mood to hash out her feelings.

She rarely talked about her past. Couldn't talk about parts of it, as Blade had verified.

She'd opened herself up for this particular chat, though. She'd let the man slip past her guard. Okay, okay. She'd all but dragged him into bed with her last night. Somewhere along the line the prickly irritation Clint Black stirred in her had morphed into an entirely different kind of itch. If Gorsky hadn't called when he did…

To her profound disgust, the mere thought of what could have happened sent ripples of regret all through her. Calling herself ten kinds of an idiot, she wedged into the corner of her seat. Despite the early departure, a good number of sleepy-eyed travelers occupied the other seats. None sat close enough to hear a casual conversation over the whine of the train's powerful electric engines, however.

When they pulled out of the station, St. Petersburg's brief night had already given way to a dawn partially obscured by angry clouds. The train picked up speed and racketed over several bridges. Soon it was whizzing past square, featureless high-rises and streets just coming awake with delivery vans and electric trolleys. After handing their tickets to the conductor, Rebel angled so she could stretch out her legs. She wore jeans again, paired with a long-sleeved navy top and the silver spangled ballet shoes. Blade was also in jeans, but his were softer and more worn—which she couldn't help but note when they bumped knees.

Her faint hope he wouldn't pursue their earlier conversation died when he reminded her they had seven and a half hours to kill before they reached Kaliningrad.

"Plenty of time for you to explain why you iced up at the hotel."

"It won't take anywhere near that long."

"I'm listening."

She made a face, hating to admit her biggest failure in life. So far, anyway.

"I was married—briefly—to a man with your brand of sex appeal."

"And what brand is that exactly?"

"The kind that makes women think evil thoughts even before you aim one of your patented, come-and-get-me grins at them."

He actually managed to look hurt. "They're not patented. I applied, but the powers that decide such weighty matters didn't agree 'come and get me' constituted a new or useful process."

She drew up a knee and dug her heel into his inner thigh. "You want to hear this or not?"

"Sorry." Capturing her ankle, he relieved the pressure. "Go on."

"Steve didn't go looking for them. I'll give him that. He just turned on the charm and they swarmed him. Unfortunately, he forgot to turn it off a time or three."

"I get the picture," Blade said, nodding. "Because your husband cheated, you think all men are scum."

"Not all men."

"Right. Only us studs."

"Not all studs, either. I can think of a dozen genuine hotties who don't emit your kind of vibes. Nick Jensen comes immediately to mind. Adam Ridgeway, too. Both of them have eyes only for their wives."

He appeared to consider that unassailable argument. "I see only one fallacy in your logic," he said after a moment.

"What's that?"

"We're not married, engaged or otherwise attached."

"True, but…"

"And if we were," he interrupted, "you could trust me."

His tone was lazy, almost casual, but the glint in his eyes suggested he might be a little pissed.

"If you don't believe me," he added in that same deceptively mild tone, "we can put the matter to a test."

"How?" she asked, wary now.

"We pick up where we left off in St. Petersburg. See where it leads."

"I…uh…"

"What's the matter, Talbot? Afraid your theory won't hold water?"

"No." Her chin came up. "I'm merely thinking of the potential complications to our mission."

"So we wait until after the mission." His thumb circled her ankle bone. "I'd better warn you, though. This vibe business works both ways. Once I stake a claim, I tend to get territorial."

Stake a claim? Get territorial? Rebel couldn't figure out how the heck this conversation had deteriorated from perfectly rational to Neanderthal. Or why the hand circling her ankle suddenly felt like a shackle. Irritated by the feeling, she tugged free of his hold.

"I'm too tired to open a whole new discussion on tests and territories. We can broach those topics another time. Right now I'm going to catch up on my sleep."

They'd do more than broach the topics, Blade thought as she curled into the corner of her seat. They'd damned well seal the deal. He eased back and divided his attention between the gray, drizzly scene whizzing by outside the windows and the woman who sank deeper into unconsciousness with each kilometer.

She woke briefly during the stop in Riga, the capital of Latvia. And again when a vendor came through the car selling cigarettes, sandwiches, potato soup, orangeade, tea and vodka. The soup was only lukewarm but the sandwiches consisted of jaw-cracking slabs of smoked ham stacked between equally thick slices of rye bread. Blade demolished all of his sandwich and the half of Rebel's that she couldn't finish.

She slipped back into a doze after lunch. He filled in the final hours of the trip skimming the last chapters of the book Professor Dawson had loaned them. The authors provided a wealth of documentation concerning the last known sightings of the Amber Room. A grainy, black-and-white photo showed it on display in Königsberg Castle. Returned, as Hitler had demanded, to its

Prussian-slash-German roots. Several eyewitnesses verified that the panels were taken down, packed into twenty-six crates, and stored for safekeeping in the castle's cellars after the first Allied bombing attack in August 1944. Only one witness, however, claimed to have seen these same crates brought up from the cellars and loaded onto a train in the last, frantic days before the Soviet Army stormed into Königsberg.

A succession of search teams could find no evidence to support this claim. More to the point, in-depth study of the last trains to have departed Königsberg showed the panels couldn't have made it out of the city ahead of the advancing Red Army. All train routes had been cut off by then. That meant the priceless amber room had either been destroyed by the bombs that had rained down on the city in the closing months of the war or— less likely, according to the authors—they'd been so well hidden that none of the subsequent search parties digging through the rubble could find them.

No one except, maybe, a saboteur crawling through sewers and underground passages. Blade shut the book and considered the possibilities. If Sergeant Thomas Bauer had stumbled onto the priceless panels, why hadn't he told anyone? Maybe he planned to go back after the war and recover more of the treasure. If so, the highly publicized Nuremberg War Crimes tribunals might have scared him off. A number of looters brought to trial at Nuremberg were sentenced to stiff prison terms.

Even if Bauer hadn't planned to profit from the panels, he must have known how anxious the Soviets were to reclaim their treasure. He could have come forward at any time over the decades. Been hailed as a hero for leading a search team to the missing panels. Why keep silent?

Blade was still pondering that question when a loud thunderclap boomed just outside the windows. Rebel woke with a start and sat up, blinking at the rain now coming down in sheets.

"Where are we?"

"About a half hour out of Kaliningrad."

She squinted through the downpour at the coast barely visible in the distance. Angry waves lashed its flat, marshy shoreline and flung monster plumes of salt spray into the air.

"Any word from Tank?" she asked, dragging her gaze from the storm-tossed sea.

"He's made hotel reservations. Also confirmed the address and phone number of Sergeant Bauer's cousin. I figured we'd wait to contact her until we checked in and dumped our bags."

Rebel nodded her agreement with that plan and made a quick trip to the WC. When she returned to her seat, the track had curved away from the coast and now arrowed south through flat farmland. Shortly after that, they entered Kaliningrad's suburbs. The dark, surly sky didn't show the post-WWII concrete-block buildings in the best light, but the sprawl of factories hinted at a thriving economy. Signs denoting Cadillac, Hummer and BMW plants flashed by, along with a giant manufacturing center for flat-screen TV's.

By the time they pulled into the central railroad station, the violent thunderstorm had dissipated to a steady drizzle. The temperature was considerably warmer here, so much farther south than St. Petersburg, although the breeze coming off the Baltic made Rebel glad she'd opted for the long-sleeved top.

They hailed a taxi outside the station. The Russian-made Volga came with a blue-striped towel covering its seat and a burly driver who insisted on acting as their tour guide.

"I show you Old City first. Then we go to hotel."

Leaning on the horn, he whipped around a plaza he identified as Victory Square and shot past a clanging trolley. A bridge took them across the Pregel River, lined on both banks with ocean-going cargo vessels. A reconstructed redbrick gate sprouting turrets and battlements led to the pre-WWII city center.

The area consisted of parks and broad avenues of lime-green linden trees. Dominating the center was the restored cathedral and a twenty-story concrete box. The box was painted an incongruous pale blue. Many of its windows were boarded, others gave glimpses into an empty interior.

"Is House of Soviets," their driver announced. "Ugliest building in all Russia."

He wouldn't get any argument there.

"House never finished. The ground beneath, she sinks."

He took both hands off the wheel to pantomime a cave-in. Rebel vacillated between an avid interest in the parliament house built atop the collapsed tunnels of Königsberg Castle and the certainty their taxi was going to plow through the barricades cordoning off the abandoned structure. The umbrella-toting pedestrians on the sidewalk in front of the barricades evidently shared the same concern. Those in the direct line of fire shouted curses and leaped aside.

Their driver reclaimed the wheel in the nick of time and swerved back into traffic. Blowing out a relieved breath, Rebel threw a look over her shoulder. Most of the pedestrians had disappeared under their umbrellas again, although one was furious enough to stand in the drizzle and flip them the bird.

Something about him...

She angled around for a better look. The drizzle clouded the windows, then a tram clanged by and obscured the plaza. She was still trying to put a name or a place to the briefly glimpsed face when the taxi shot around a corner and down another tree-lined boulevard.

"Is Amber Museum."

Their self-appointed guide jabbed a thumb at a squat, redbrick tower directly ahead. The tower must once have formed part of the medieval city walls. Now, apparently, it housed one of Kaliningrad's premier tourists attractions.

"Best museum in city."

Rebel marked the location in her mind. From her reading, she knew the museum housed an exhibition depicting the history of the room that had originated right here, in what had once been East Prussia. It might be worth a visit if Thomas Bauer's cousin didn't come through for them.

Contacting Clara Bauer Soloff constituted their first priority after checking into the hotel. They didn't get adjoining rooms this time. Rebel waffled between relief and disappointment when Blade left her at her door with a promise to return as soon as he'd cleaned up and checked in with Tank.

She used the brief interval to splash water on her face and drag a brush through her hair. A few swipes of lip gloss made her feel almost feminine again. She debated whether to change out of her jeans for the visit to Bauer's cousin but decided to wait until they'd fixed a time and a place.

Blade rapped on her door a few minutes later. He'd grabbed a quick shower, she noted when she opened her door. His hair gleamed dark and damp. He'd also shaved. The tantalizing scent of leather and lime teased Rebel as she brushed past him and retrieved her phone from her purse.

"Let's see if we can track down this cousin."

The task almost maxed out her linguistic skills, but she eventually ascertained that the phone number and address Tank had supplied was for a retirement home, not a private residence. The attendant Rebel spoke to indicated Ms. Soloff's son had taken her into the country for some kind of family celebration. They expected her to return by noon tomorrow.

She left her name and number and said she would come by to visit Ms. Soloff early tomorrow afternoon. Swallowing her frustration, she flipped her phone shut.

"Looks like we have the rest of the day to kill."

And night.

The thought landed with a thud. She could tell by the glint in Blade's eyes it had hit him, too. For a heart-stopping second, she actually considered the possibilities.

Talk about going from one extreme to the other! All this time she'd kicked herself for falling in love with a handsome charmer who couldn't keep his pants zipped. Now here she was, in serious lust with another super stud who dared her to put him to the test.

The nasty suspicion she might have let Clint Black's exterior blind her to the man inside irritated her no end. It also made her absurdly nervous. She squashed both emotions with a casual suggestion.

"That Amber Museum is only a few blocks from here. Why don't we check it out?"

They exited the hotel and discovered that weak but struggling sunlight had vanquished the rain. It had also nudged the July temperature up from comfortable to downright muggy. Storefront canopies dripped on them as they walked. Sidewalk puddles steamed. Rebel could almost feel her hair frizzing in the few short blocks to the redbrick tower.

As they walked, she couldn't help glancing at the passersby. She still couldn't place the guy who'd flipped them the bird. She'd caught only a glimpse of his face, and that had been distorted by drizzle and her profound relief their cab driver hadn't flattened him. Something about him nagged at her, though. She was damned if she knew what.

"Careful!"

Blade caught her elbow and kept her from stepping off the curb in the path of an approaching tram.

"Reminds me of my home town," he commented as the trolley rattled past.

Some passengers were jammed shoulder-to-shoulder. Others hanging on the outer steps. Rebel ignored them to give the man beside her a curious look.

"You're from San Francisco?"

"Not originally, but I spent enough time there to qualify as a native."

Why didn't she know that? The gap in her knowledge bugged her as they crossed the busy street. She added it to the other questions she'd compiled about this man in the past few days. At the top of the list was the question of who he'd cut, and why. She toyed with the idea of asking him outright but nixed the impulse. This wasn't the time or the place. Besides, she wasn't sure he'd tell her. Parts of his past had to be as shrouded in secrecy as hers.

She was pondering that distinct possibility as they approached the round tower housing the Amber Museum. The darkened windows gave them their first clue it might not be open. The hand-lettered sign stuck in the door provided another.

"Can you read it?" Blade asked.

"I'm not sure."

She struggled with the Cyrillic lettering. She could speak Russian with some fluency. Reading it was another matter. Particularly when the letters were written in a spidery script adorned with an overabundance of curlicues.

"I think it says something about the storm."

"Maybe the lightning knocked out their lights."

"Maybe."

She was still trying to decipher the cryptic message when a teenager with a profusion of ear and nose rings wheeled up on a skateboard.

"Museum is closed," he confirmed in Russian.

"Yes, I see. Why?"

Heeling his board, he skidded to a stop. "You are English?"

"American."

"Ahhh!" His eyes lit up. "CKY. Pearl Jam. You know them?"

When Rebel hummed the first few bars of *Just Breathe,* the kid followed her lead and launched into an ecstatic rendition of the recently re-released hit.

Not until they'd finished their impromptu duet did she discover why the museum's lights were out.

"The storm churns the sea," the teenager explained. "Waves wash amber ashore. The museum director goes to Yantarny to collect it, along with half of Kaliningrad."

"Yantarny?"

"It is where amber was mined for many years." He gestured vaguely toward the coast. "Twenty, thirty kilometers from here."

Chapter 7

The idea of hunting for amber in its natural state proved impossible to resist. Rebel convinced Blade they should hail another taxi and gave Yantarny as their destination. The route took them past miles of marshy fields and the abandoned hangars of a former Soviet air base. In the distance, the pearl-colored Baltic rippled with lines of whitecaps.

The sun burned through the last of the cloud cover as they approached Yantarny. The faded resort town occupied the very tip of a broad peninsula surrounded on three sides by the Baltic. A handful of weather-beaten hotels with wide verandas hugged the scraggly shoreline. Restaurants displayed barely legible signs, their lettering sanded off by years of salt-laden winds. Old men with cigarettes dangling from their lips hunched on the beach next to thick-waisted women in babushkas. The older generation watched as their offspring waded through the surf. Some of the waders wielded nets. One enterprising couple appeared to be swishing tennis rackets through the rippling surf.

"I read about this," Rebel exclaimed after they'd exited the taxi and felt the wind slap their faces. "During a storm, the violent action of waves disturbs the seabed. Millions of years worth of buried gunk gets stirred up, including fossilized amber that was formed when conifer forests covered this whole area."

The air carried the nose-twitching tang of salt and damp, verdant marsh. Breathing both into her lungs, Rebel put up a hand to hold back her wind-whipped hair.

"When the Teutonic Knights controlled the amber trade, they forced their harvesters to wade far out into the sea after storms to scoop stuff up with nets. Hundreds supposedly drowned in the icy water. And the knights reportedly executed anyone they caught sneaking out at night to do a little private scooping."

She turned in a slow semicircle, searching the shore and the low, chalky cliffs behind them.

"Harvesting continued right up to modern times. There's a huge amber mine around here somewhere. It operated until 2002 or 2003, if I remember correctly."

"That's probably where the workers at Catherine

Palace got the materials to replicate the original room,"
Blade commented.

"Probably."

She eyed the crowd shuffling ankle deep through
the surf and couldn't resist issuing a challenge.

"Bet I turn up a piece of amber before you do."

"You sure you want to dive in?" he asked skeptically.
"The air temperature may be in the seventies, but I'm
guessing the water's a good twenty degrees colder."

A familiar light entered her eyes. Blade recognized
the mocking glint even before she pantomimed flapping wings.

"Cluck, cluck, cluck."

"I'm not chicken. Just sensible."

"Forget sensible. Let's have some fun."

He entertained serious doubts as he followed her
down to the beach, where she slipped off her span-
gly shoes and rolled up her jeans. Stuffing the shoes
in her back pockets, she approached the water's edge.
Blade decided discretion was the better part of valor
and waited for the first wave to hit her.

"Omigod!"

Yelping, she leaped for dry land. He caught her hand
and tugged her free of the sucking surf. Her shocked
expression brought laughter rumbling up in his chest.
Nobly, he resisted the urge to say he told her so, but the
evil look she gave the waves had him grinning.

"Now who's chicken?"

"At least I went in!"

She tugged free of his hold and made a cautious re-entry. Her lips peeled back in a grimace. Her shoulders hunched, as if she wanted them to lift her bodily out of the water. Step by excruciating step, she waded in up to her calves. Moments later she'd joined the other hunter-gatherers sloshing through seaweed, pebbles and flotsam in search of bits of prehistoric resin.

The wind tangled her hair and flattened her top against her breasts. Seawater splashed up to her thighs. Mesmerized, Blade watched a Rebel he'd never seen before dance away from another wave.

The woman had roused his interest, then his lust, from the first day they'd met. She'd challenged him. Taunted him. Stirred his competitive instincts. Yet this was the first time he'd glimpsed this laughing, carefree side to her.

"Our bet's still on," she called over her shoulder. "You coming in or not?"

"Not."

"Cluck, cluck, cluck."

"You mine the waves. I'll comb the beach."

He paced her from higher up on the shore as she splashed through knee-high surf. They occasioned a few curious glances from the other hunters but were ignored by most until Rebel gave an excited shout.

"I see something!"

She bowled her hands and bent to scoop up her find. Wind and excitement put flags of color in her cheeks as she straightened and let seawater seep through her fingers.

Several of her fellow hunters waded closer for a look. One of them took the oblong piece she displayed in her outstretched palm and chinked it against his teeth. Shaking his head, he passed it back to her.

"Nyet."

Obviously disappointed, Rebel resumed her search. Blade trailed along, alternating his gaze between the ebbing tide and the tawny-haired sea witch who roused the erotic and totally implausible urge to drag her down to the sand and recreate the famous beach scene in *From Here to Eternity.* He had her wet and willing and panting with eagerness when he spotted a dull glint half buried in seaweed.

Hunkering down, he brushed kelp away from an irregularly shaped blob about the size of a half dollar. He dug it out and swished it through the surf to remove the grit and sand. It felt almost weightless, more like plastic than a semiprecious gem. If it *was* a semiprecious gem. Blade still wasn't convinced when Rebel splashed over to see what he'd found.

"Omigod," she said again, more reverently this time. "Look at that amazing color."

The piece glowed a rich golden-brown. Its surface undulated in uneven planes. Tiny bubbles dotted one corner and what looked like a miniature fern unfurled just off center. The piece was pretty, Blade had to admit, but he had no clue whether it was the real thing.

The Russians who gathered around them seemed to think so. One conducted the teeth knocking test again. Another rubbed the piece vigorously against the arm of his bulky sweater and held it an inch or so from Rebel's head. Strands of her hair flew up, as if drawn by a magnet. Grinning, she translated a babble of comments.

"They say it's the real thing."

"Better ask them about the rules governing finds like this. We may have to report it or something."

The question elicited shrugs all around and a return to the business of treasure hunting.

"We can ask at the museum tomorrow," Rebel said. "Assuming the amber police don't come knocking on your door first and confiscate the piece." She glided a fingertip along the uneven surface. "Be a shame if they do. This would make a gorgeous pendant or belt buckle."

Blade nodded but had something besides jewelry on his mind at the moment. "You know," he said with studied nonchalance, "we didn't set the stakes for that bet about who would find amber first."

The too-lazy tone brought her gaze up to lock his. "No," she said cautiously, "we didn't."

"Guess that means the winner gets to name the prize."

"Within reason."

His gaze made a leisurely descent from her tangled hair to her mouth to the front of her long-sleeved navy top. The surf had splotched and dampened the stretchy material. It now outlined her breasts in precise detail. The need to cup those high, taut mounds jolted into Blade. He managed to refrain but not without considerable struggle.

Yielding to another, equally compelling urge, he slid a hand under the heavy mass of her hair. Her nape felt warm and slightly damp from her exertions. Her skin carried the tang of the sea.

"I'll take this as a down payment on my prize."

Her expression went from cautious to wary but she didn't pull back. They were making real progress, Blade thought as he bent and brushed his mouth over hers. Moving from friendly adversaries to…

To what? The question rode roughshod over the pleasure of her taste and feel and damp, salty scent. When he raised his head, she opened her eyes and blinked at the frown he felt forming.

"What?" she demanded, bristling a little at his sudden change of mood.

"Funny," he said slowly, "I was just asking myself the same thing."

"Huh?"

His gaze roamed her face, but he knew the answer to his question even before he catalogued the rich cinnamon of her eyes, the thick lashes, the lush mouth and stubborn chin. He ached for her in the most basic way a man could for a woman. So fiercely it took every ounce of his control not to drag her down and do the Burt Lancaster thing.

But he wanted more than a roll in the sand, he real-ized with an unwelcome jolt. He wanted her laughing as she had a few minutes ago. Lighthearted. Loving him as much as…

Whoa! His thoughts slammed to a full stop. When the hell had he tripped over lust and come down some-where close to love? The idea scared the crap out of him even as he bent to take her lips again. Harder this time. Hungrier.

Rebel stood stiff and unresponsive for a few seconds, still more than a little miffed. What the heck was going on here? One minute he was teasing her with that evil grin of his. The next, he was looking as freaked as an armadillo caught in the headlights.

And now his stance had widened, his hand had tun-neled through her hair and he was coaxing—correc-tion!—*demanding* a response. She wanted to withhold it. That near scowl when he'd raised his head a minute ago still stung. Like she'd insisted on partial payment right here on the beach, with an interested audience looking on.

But he felt so good. Tasted so good. Against her better judgment, almost against her will, she slid her arms around his neck. She had no idea how long they would have remained locked like that if someone hadn't given a snarky laugh and offered the Russian version of "get a room."

Breaking the kiss, she lowered her arms and leaned back in Blade's loose hold. "What was that all about?"

A line of red cut across his cheeks. "Damned if I know."

The red deepened, and Rebel's jaw sagged. Good grief! Was that a blush? Her first instinct was to hoot and tease the hell out of him. She wasn't sure what held her back. Sheer surprise, maybe, or the sudden and totally ridiculous stutter in her pulse. Whatever the reason, she decided not to ruin the moment with one of her usual barbs.

"Well, when you figure it out," she said instead, "let me in on it."

Pushing out of his hold, she resumed her wading and pretended not to hear his growled, "You'll be the first to know."

Acclimated to the surf's chill now, she led the way along the curving the shoreline. The crowd thinned out the farther they got from the hotels and restaurants. Instead of eager amber hunters, the few folks along this deserted stretch were mostly loners out for a walk and the occasional elderly gull-watcher bundled in a thick sweater or jacket despite the reappearing sun.

Rebel nodded and smiled at several, with mixed results. Russia's postwar generation might be relatively receptive to strangers but many of their older counterparts still regarded outsiders with Cold War suspicion. She was hoping Sergeant Bauer's elderly cousin wasn't one of them, when she and Blade rounded a curve in the shoreline and found their way blocked by a low chalk cliff that jutted into the sea.

Except it wasn't a chalk cliff, she realized as they moved closer. It was a man-made extrusion some hundred or so yards long made from heaps of gray slag. Massive pipes so rusty they showed daylight through their holes lay half submerged on either side of the extrusion. An equally rusted structure of corrugated tin sat at the tip.

Curious, Rebel abandoned the water and leaned on Blade to swipe the sand from her feet before slipping on her shoes. Dusting her hands on her thighs, she approached a sign with an official-looking seal. Time and salt spray had all but obliterated the lettering.

"I wonder…"

Hands on hips, she followed the line of one of the half-submerged pipes from where it emerged from the water some yards ahead. The rusting pipe lay across the beach like the carcass of a bloated sea serpent, then penetrated a crumbling wall and led up a slight incline to a long, low cement building almost obscured by weeds.

"What's that?" Blade asked, following her gaze.

"I'm not sure."

"Could be an antiship or aircraft battery left over from the war," he speculated.

"Could be," Rebel agreed. "But I think…"

She turned, spotted a white-haired man sitting on the wall, and motioned to Blade to follow her. With the old man's shoulders hunched and a thin black cigarette stuck to his lower lip, he could have been part of the crumbling ruins. A threadbare army overcoat with red pips on the tabs was draped over his shoulders. Two faded medals hung on the right lapel below a face so weathered and lined it seemed to have folded back in on itself.

"Excuse me," Rebel said in polite Russian. "We don't want to trespass, but the sign is too faded to read. Do you know what it says?"

He looked at her through narrowed eyes for so long she thought he wouldn't answer. "It says to have care," he finally croaked in a hoarse, smoke-roughened voice. "The mine is abandoned. Unsafe."

Her pulse kicked up a notch. She'd suspected the slag heap might be the by-product from the mine she'd read about. This hunch-shouldered veteran had just validated her guess.

"Thank you."

The old man grunted and returned to his contemplation of the sea.

"I think this is the amber mine," Rebel interpreted for Blade. "The one that operated until just a few years ago."

Her hair whipping wildly, she dug in the purse hooked across her body and nudged aside her snub-nosed .38 to extract her phone. A single click took her to the internet. Another few clicks brought up a Wiki-pedia article on the Yantarny Amber Mine.

"Ha! I was right. It says here this sucker's been in operation for centuries." She scrolled through the article, hitting the highlights. "The Prussians took over the lucrative amber trade when the Teutonic Knights were disbanded. Amber collected all along this coastline was brought here to Yantarny for processing, then sent to Königsberg."

"Where Fredrick the Whatever's court architect discovered a whole cellar full and crafted a room out of it," Blade commented.

"Fredrick the First," she supplied, skimming the article. "According to this, the Prussians leased production in 1818 to a private firm. The firm operated the biggest and most profitable amber mine in the world, right up until it got flooded out in 2001."

Rebel wasn't sure why finding the abandoned mine was so exciting. Probably because it constituted one more piece in what had become a frustrating puzzle. Eagerly, she scrolled through the article.

"The Yantarny Mine was incredibly rich. By 1937 it employed over a thousand people and produced more than six hundred tons of amber a year. Then, in 1945…"

She broke off, pursing her lips.

"In 1945," Blade filled in, "the Soviets invaded."

"Right. But first…"

Her excitement faded. A sick feeling stirred in its stead.

"There was a Nazi concentration camp outside Danzig, Poland. When the Soviet Army advanced in January 1945, the camp's guards forced more than thirteen thousand inmates to march through hundreds of miles of snow and sleet to Königsberg, then out here to the coast. Less than three thousand survived the march."

Her sick feeling intensified as she read the next paragraph.

"The plan was to imprison the survivors in one of the mine's tunnels. But the mine manager objected, so the prisoners were forced into the Baltic and machine gunned."

Blade turned his gaze to the waves rolling onto the shore. "Makes you see this place in a different light," he said grimly.

"Yeah, it does."

Rebel had studied thousands of years of military history at the Air Force Academy, from Egypt's earliest warrior kings to the Greeks and Romans and Carthaginians, down through the Middle Ages to modern times. She knew atrocities were committed by all sides in every conflict. She also knew there were those who argued dropping atomic bombs on Hiroshima and Nagasaki constituted mass murder of innocent noncombatants. That didn't lessen the impact of what she'd just read. It took a severe effort of will to force her mind away from the horror that had taken place in the waters just yards away.

"The tunnels mentioned in the article," she said slowly. "They had to have been created when the mine operators dredged down to reach amber buried in the seabed."

"And once they reached it," Blade commented,

studying the mountain of gray sludge projecting into the sea, "they had to have some way to separate the good stuff from the bad. I'm guessing they used high pressure spray guns powered with seawater."

Rebel tried to visualize the process in her mind. She saw shafts sunk deep into the marshy earth. Tons upon tons of dark, slimy seabed scooped up by dredges. Dumped onto conveyors and hauled through a processing plant. Attacked by high pressure sprays that sluiced mud from wood and stone and clumps of prehistoric resin.

The clumps were separated and probably treated with some kind of chemical to wash off encrustations. Effluvia from the process would be pumped through giant pipes back down into the sea. No wonder this stretch of the Baltic looked barren and gray!

"And then," she said, thinking out loud, "mine operators had to ship the finished product to a sorting, grading, and wholesaling center. In Königsberg, I would guess. The question now is…"

"How they shipped it," Blade finished. He studied the plant's long, low facade. "You said the mine was producing six hundred tons of amber a year in 1937. Trucking it out would be too inefficient. I'm guessing a railroad spur."

Another flare of excitement kindled as Rebel remembered the eyewitness who'd insisted he'd seen the crated Amber Room panels loaded onto a train in late April 1945. Exhaustive research had proved no train could have left Königsberg and headed north, west or south by that date. The city was already almost surrounded.

But one could have steamed here, hauling priceless amber panels back to the mine that produced them so many centuries ago. The breath-stealing possibility had her scanning the overgrown areas in front and alongside the plant.

"I don't see any tracks."

"You wouldn't from down here," Blade countered. "Let's go up and take a look."

They had to search for the weed-clogged track that led up from the beach. Rebel half expected the old soldier to shout an order to stop, or at least issue another warning that the mine wasn't safe. He did neither, merely flicked them a disinterested glance and went back to his contemplation of the sea.

The stink of long-standing water turned sour and brackish, clogging Rebel's nostrils as they got closer to the abandoned plant. She stepped lightly, cautiously, her enthusiasm for the search dimming as she tried not to think about an abandoned shaft opening up under her feet or stepping into a sinkhole of gray, viscous sludge.

When she and Blade gained the top of the rise they saw concrete building had once been ringed with barbed wire. The strands were now rusted and the fence had toppled into the scrub in several places. They got through it easily enough and approached what must have been the long, low processing plant.

The gray cinderblock facility looked even worse up

close than it had from the shore. Boards were nailed haphazardly across windows. Rusting iron bars blocked the door. Wind and relentless sea spray had pockmarked the walls and eaten off big chunks of cement. Treading even more cautiously, Rebel followed in Blade's footsteps as he searched for tracks in the weeds and refuse lining the length of building.

"Nothing here. Let's look around back."

"You look. I'll wait."

He glanced over his shoulder and caught her making a face as she unwrapped a prickly weed that had snaked around her ankle. Grinning, he flapped his wings.

"Cluck, cluck."

He'd rounded the corner before Rebel could think of an appropriate response. With another moue of distaste she retraced her steps. She didn't mind getting grungy in the line of duty. If she'd had any squeamishness about that left after four years at the academy, her subsequent Survival, Evasion, Resistance and Escape training would have eradicated it. And even SERE paled in comparison with some of her less savory experiences as an OMEGA agent. Like that never-to-be-forgotten belly crawl through an oil-polluted swamp glutted with dead fish.

Grimacing at the memory, Rebel made her way back along the length of the building. Its elevation gave a clear view down the slope leading down the gray slag mound. Behind her, the long rows of boarded windows and barred doors seemed to mock her brief spurt of optimism.

Just enough of that optimism remained for her to edge closer to a window and squint through a crack in the boards. She couldn't see a thing. Stepping back, she eyed the rusting nails holding the boards in place and decided she had nothing to lose by giving one of them a yank.

Except her dignity, she discovered when nails screeched and a rotting board jerked free in her hands. Light poured into the dark interior. A second later, bats poured out. Big, nasty, flapping, whirring, squealing bats.

Rebel yelped and dropped to her knees. She stayed there, protecting her head with her arms, while the seemingly endless black cloud battered and bruised the air above her.

Chapter 8

Once the cloud of bats whirred off, Rebel felt brave enough to pry off a few more boards. Not brave enough to climb through the window, however, until Blade returned. Maybe not even then.

She fished out her comm device, switched on its high-powered laser, and aimed the beam around the interior. The light barely penetrated the gloom. After several futile minutes, she switched off the beam.

Hopefully, Blade would find traces of rail tracks buried in the weeds at the rear of the building. They wouldn't prove anything, of course. Just raise the interesting possibility that the curators of the heavily bombed Königsberg Castle *could* have trundled the priceless Amber Room panels out here to the Yantarny Mine for safekeeping.

"Find anything?" she asked when he reappeared.

"No railroad tracks, but something almost as interesting." He eyed the gaping hole in the window. "How about you?"

"Winged creatures." She couldn't quite repress a shudder. "Lots of them. They burst out in swarms."

"Which begs the question," he said thoughtfully, "of how they got in. I'll take a look."

She was tempted to let him swing a leg over the sill and go it alone. The idea he might disturb another screeching, flapping dark cloud seriously creeped her out. She could almost feel nasty little claws tangling in her hair. All those sharp, rabies-carrying fangs sinking into her skin. Wondering why in the world devotees of vampire novels thought those bloodsuckers were sexy, she edged to the window and gave herself a muttered pep talk.

"You can do this. You scared them worse than they scared you. They're gone. Not coming back."

Besides, she couldn't let her partner go in without backup. Or worse, let him see this girly side of her. Not that Blade would hold her bat-o-phobia over her. Or maybe he would. She wouldn't put it past him to exploit this tiny chink in her armor.

The memory of their subtle and not-so subtle clashes over the years got her through the window. But the reassuring sight of his broad-shouldered figure fired a rush of more recent memories. Most notably those moments tangled in the sheets back in the St. Petersburg hotel and the lingering aftershocks of their kiss on the beach a little while ago. Ricocheting back and forth between her feelings toward the old and the new Blade, she followed him into a dark, dank cavern as long as a football field.

The stink was stronger inside. Sulfur, Rebel thought, her nose twitching, overlaid with damp and years of rot. Barely enough light came through the window to illuminate the layers of gray dust coating the entire interior. Blade switched on his beam, Rebel did hers, and still they could make out only dim shapes and shadow. The building had obviously been stripped of all usable or recyclable equipment, but they spotted what looked like the remains of a conveyor system toppled over onto its side. Above it was a series of rusted metal vats, some with crooked spouts hanging from them.

"This must have been a processing area," Blade guessed. "Probably where they used chemicals to wash the sludge off the amber brought up from the mine shafts."

Rebel nodded, too occupied with checking the rafters above the vats for hanging critters to comment.

The light from the window didn't pierce the inky darkness at either end of the long building but did show what looked like abandoned offices across from where they stood. Doors hung crookedly on hinges eroded by the salt air. A faint spear of light came through a central door that obviously gave onto the outside.

Blade squinted at the gloom to his far left, then right. "We need to come back with higher-powered flashlights. But you have to see this before we go."

Whatever "this" was. He steered her around the toppled conveyor toward the outside door on the far side. When he raised a foot and sent the door back on its hinges, Rebel instinctively hunched her shoulders. No squeaking, eeking swarm descended. Even so, she didn't draw a full breath until she was through the door and back in the sunlight.

Her breath whooshed out again at the sight that greeted her. They were standing almost on the rim of a monster crater. It wasn't deep, but looked to be several miles across. Stunted trees with bare, twisted limbs dotted the ridge and sides of the bowl. A sea of gray sludge coated its bottom.

"This is it," she breathed. "This is the pit where they bored down into seabed to bring up amber."

She followed the crater's circumference and spotted the rusted remains of what might have been an excavator tower about a quarter way around. A little beyond that was the gaping mouth of one of the pipes that carried waste down to the sea.

She turned in a slow circle, still following the circumference. She'd almost made it back to where they stood when she gasped. There, nearly obscured by weeds, was a caved-in section of the crater's wall.

Beyond the crumbled section Rebel could just glimpse rotting, tilted timbers.

"Is that a tunnel?"

"Looks like it," Blade confirmed.

She edged closer to the rim and peered over the side. "It had to have led to this building."

"That would be my guess. We can check it out when we come back with those flashlights."

The old soldier was gone when they descended what Rebel now knew was the sloping wall of the Yantarny Mine crater. Too bad. Although he hadn't exactly gone out of his way to be friendly, she would have liked to ask him more about the mine.

When they neared the smattering of hotels and restaurants, she saw the crowd wading through the surf had thinned out, as well. Many must have decided to thaw out in the hotels' bars and restaurants. Or so it seemed when Rebel and Blade walked into a two-story hotel fronted by a sagging wooden veranda.

The cloud of cigarette smoke flavored with the tantalizing scent of onions and fried fish made her realize the Baltic's long summer days had given her a false sense of time. It also made her stomach sit up and take immediate notice. A warning rumble reminded her it hadn't been fed since the ham-on-rye sandwich aboard the train.

"I'm starved. Let's eat here."

Blade eyed the thick smoke and shrugged. He'd eaten in worse places. So, evidently, had Rebel. She held up two fingers to the aproned waitress who came to seat them and smiled her acquiescence when the woman showed them to a table by the window. Blade started to do the same but caught himself just in time. Face set, he slid into his seat.

Dammit all to hell! He couldn't believe he'd let Rebel's pointed remarks about his nonverbal signals sneak into his psyche. Thoroughly irritated, he glanced up and caught her smirk.

"What's the matter? The waitress isn't your type?"

"Keep this up," he snapped, "and I'll be forced to show you exactly what my type is."

She laughed at the threat, which only added to his annoyance.

"Want me to order for you?"

He nodded, in no way ready to admit she'd dinged his subconscious. She was ready when the waitress came back with menus. The woman didn't so much as glance at Blade.

"What are we having?" he asked when she departed.

"I broke one of my own rules and ordered the local beer along with two servings of Königsberg *klopse.* Meatballs boiled in salt water," Rebel translated, "then cooked in a sauce with onions, white pepper and capers. I heard about them when I was stationed in Moscow but never got to sample the originals."

The originals, they discovered a short time later, more than lived up to their hype. The succulent meatballs were served with boiled potatoes and the inevitable beets. Even those, Blade had to admit, tasted pretty good when washed down with the local beer. The lager's dark gold color reminded him of the riches mined from the restless sea outside the windows

He drained the rest of his beer and slid his hand in his pocket. He fingered the piece he'd scavenged, imagining how it would look set in silver and draped around Rebel's throat. Or mounted on a wide bracelet that would lock around her wrist. Better yet, her ankle.

He could see her naked, wearing nothing but his cuff on one slender ankle. So proud. So defiant. Refusing to admit he'd marked her as his. The atavistic image speared in him like a hot poker.

It was still burning in his gut when the taxi dropped them at their hotel an hour or so later. He knew that was no excuse. Knew he should ride up in the elevator with her, leave her at her door and walk away. And he would have. He was sure of it. If she hadn't spotted the amber display in the window of the hotel's tiny gift shop.

"Look! There's a piece about the same size and shape as the one you found." She had to stop for a closer look. "Good grief!"

Blade still might have managed to keep his hands to himself if she hadn't hooked her hair behind one ear and pursed her lips in a low whistle.

"You wouldn't think this stuff would be so expensive here in Kaliningrad."

He gave up the fight at that point. In profile she looked sea reddened and wind tossed, minus any kind of makeup or war paint. He didn't fool himself into thinking that meant he was seeing the real Victoria Talbot. He knew she possessed layers she hadn't shared—couldn't share—with him. Nuances to her personality he hadn't yet experienced. But the laughing, carefree woman he'd glimpsed on the beach this afternoon had delivered a powerhouse punch to his solar plexus. And the one he wanted to adorn with amber was shredding what was left of his common sense.

He didn't jump her. He gave himself credit for that much, at least. He walked her down the hall to her room and waited until she keyed the lock to make his move.

"You remember our discussion on the train this afternoon? The one about waiting to pick up where we left off in St. Petersburg?"

Her eyes went wary. "I remember."

"I've changed my mind."

"About which part?"

"The waiting part." He laid his other palm against the door, caging her. "I told you the next time I got you naked, I wasn't going to keep one eye on the clock. We don't meet with Bauer's cousin until tomorrow afternoon."

His voice roughened. He let her hear the desire, wanted her to see it when he smiled a slow challenge.

"We've got all night, Talbot. All morning."

She cocked a brow. "Is that your subtle way of letting me know you can last all night? And all morning?"

His smile widened. "Try me."

The sheer arrogance of that grin took Rebel's breath away. She ached to knock the male smugness off his face. And what better way to do it than by taking up his challenge? She recognized how pitiful that rationale was even as the erotic possibilities exploded inside her head.

"You're on."

That was all he'd been waiting for. All either of them had. Blade was the one who thrust her into the room and kicked the door shut, but she was already attacking his shirt buttons. She had them half undone when he backed her against the wall. His hands were rough as he anchored her head. His mouth ground into hers.

Something hot and reckless came alive in Rebel. She reveled in the taut, muscled body pinning her to the wall. Thrilled to the savagery of his kiss. A distant corner of her mind shouted a warning. Some inanity about the danger of rousing a sleeping tiger. She ignored the shout and thrilled instead to the beast she'd roused behind his zipper. The hard bulge pressed against her belly, demanding attention.

She gave it. Hooking her calf around his for balance, she wedged the heel of her hand against his rigid length, slid it down, up, down again. His breath hissed in. His stomach hollowed. Beneath the shirt she'd half opened, his muscles felt like heated steel against hers. He caught her thigh, lifted it higher, rubbed himself against her core until Rebel went wild with need. Tearing her mouth from his, she gasped an urgent command.

"Let's have…the first demonstration of your…staying power."

Blade was ready, willing and so eager he hurt with it. Somehow he managed to keep them both upright while he freed himself and she shimmied frantically out of her jeans and panties. Just enough blood remained in his brain for him to remember a condom. Retrieving it one-handed from his back pocket proved to be another tricky maneuver.

"What are you doing?" Rebel demanded.

She got an odd look on her face when he produced the foil packet, and Blade cursed under his breath. Despite his red hot haze, he guessed instantly she was thinking of her cheating ex. Equating being prepared to being a man-whore. He was trying to marshal a coherent argument to the contrary when she surprised him with a throaty laugh.

"Hope you've got a good supply of those."

God, he hoped so, too!

He kept her backed against the wall while he sheathed himself. Rebel insisted on helping. Her hands were so urgent she damned near unstayed his staying power right there. Then the rest of his blood surged south, and he thrust up.

She closed around him, silky and tight. He'd imagined her like this, he thought before his brain shut down completely. Her face flushed, her mouth red and swollen from his kiss. With her head thrown back and her body quivering in need, she reminded him again of an untamed sea witch. A brown-eyed, amber-haired siren luring him to his fate.

Then he spotted the tiny, now-healed nick in her throat. It was almost lost in a patch of newly irritated skin. Remorse pierced Blade's red fog, slowing his hands, stiffening his back.

Her lids flew up. Eyes cloudy with desire questioned, then demanded.

"I'm marking you," he said gruffly. "I should shave."

"Do it later."

She reinforced the terse command by tightening her stomach muscles. Blade had time for a fleeting prayer of thanks for her incredibly well-toned abs before she drew him back into the vortex. Shifting her higher on his hips, he drove into her. He thought he'd choke on the effort but he managed to hold on until she came. Two heartbeats after a groan ripped from her throat, she convulsed and turned him inside out.

After that first frantic coupling, Blade dragged on his clothes and made a quick trip down the hall. His razor wasn't the only item in his shaving kit he needed to retrieve. Resupplied with enough protection to last until the drugstores opened, he got rid of his whiskers before joining Rebel in the shower. Steam fogged the glass stall while they soaped the slopes and valleys and secret places they'd been in too much of a hurry to explore before.

They toweled each other off and adjourned to the bed. Rebel's wet hair streamed across his chest, as soft and enticing as fingers of seaweed drifting on the current. They kept the pace slow this time, even when she pushed up on her knees and straddled him. Slow, that is, until her back arched and her outthrust breasts goaded him into rolling over and driving them both over the edge again.

She fell asleep with her head nested on his shoulder. Blade drew her closer, wryly aware that he wouldn't mind a few hours to recharge before making good on the rest of his boast. He was also aware that he hadn't briefed OMEGA control on their excursion to the Yantarny Amber Mine. He needed to get Tank on that. See if he could dig up some schematics that might show a record of a railroad spur. The odds were astronomical that he and Rebel had stumbled onto a possible evacuation route for the treasures once stored in Königsberg Castle but no more far-out than any of the other theories postulated by the teams that had searched for the Amber Room panels for more than six decades. With Rebel's breath warm on his neck and an abandoned tunnel filling his mind, he drifted into sleep.

Tank took the call just at 5:00 p.m. Washington time. A quick glance at the wall-mounted clocks showed him it was 9:00 a.m. in Kaliningrad.

The past twenty-four hours had been one of those long, monotonous stretches he'd been warned about. He'd tracked Blade and Rebel from St. Petersburg to the tiny wedge of Russian territory jutting into the Baltic

and confirmed they'd checked into the rooms he'd reserved for them. He'd filled the empty hours since then
by scoping out the training he'd need to complete before
going into the field.

He wasn't worried about weapons certification. His
parents had taught all three of their children to shoot
and practice strict gun safety. What's more, his brother-
in-law was an All-Service gold medalist and small
arms tactics instructor at Quantico between missions
for OMEGA. What Mike Callahan, code name Hawk,
didn't know about weapons hadn't been invented yet.

Same with defensive tactics. Tank had served as an
ADA in Philadelphia. While the City of Brotherly Love
had bred centuries of noble, upstanding citizens, it had
also spawned its share of scum. There were parts of
Philadelphia he wouldn't have ventured into without
a weapon and the confidence instilled by brutal self-
defense courses.

OMEGA's Offensive Tactics Course had him worried, though. He had to admit he hadn't previously considered either a bootlace or a wire coat hanger as lethal
weapons. He was thinking of all the ways he might
learn to strangle someone when the light on the console flashed.

"Morning," he said after Blade's biometrics cleared
him through. "You and Rebel have a good night?"

The silence at the other end of the comm link lasted
only a few seconds.

"Very good."

No fool, Tank gave a soundless whistle but kept his conclusions to himself as Blade continued.

"I need you to do some digging for us."

"Dodge warned me to keep my shovel handy 24/7."

He could hear the smile in Blade's reply.

"Good. See what you can find on the Yantarny Mine."

He spelled the name and added the interesting information that the mine had most likely provided the amber for the priceless panels a U.S. Army sergeant might or might not have located.

"I'm looking for schematics or architectural drawings with the layout of the plant," Blade related. "Also any record of rail spurs that might have connected the mine to the city of Königsberg."

"I'll start digging."

"We're meeting with Thomas Bauer's cousin at one our time," Blade reminded him. "Should be done by two or three, then we might head back out to the mine. Call me if you find anything."

"Will do."

"Thanks."

The search ate up the better part of two hours. The Russians were understandably reluctant to share information about an operation that had spewed more than a hundred million tons of waste into the Baltic before the sea itself flooded the mine and shut it down. Tank waded through the few available environmental assessments and read a grim medical report on workers who'd lost their jobs when the mine closed. Apparently, a good number of them had camped out for months at the mouths of the waste pipes, sifting for amber in the toxic effluent that seeped down from the abandoned mine until that, too, played out.

Sobered by the variety of fatal illnesses afflicting the scavengers, Tank tried a search of pre-WWII East Prussian mine operations. He got luckier there. In the late 1850s, a German by the name of Moritz Becker had apparently holidayed on the Baltic Coast near what was then Königsberg. Becker saw the locals collecting amber and formed a partnership with one Wilhelm Stantien to systematically rape the sea of its precious by-product. Becker and Stantien financed two mines. One soon proved unprofitable and was shut down. The second provided the partners untold riches until the Soviets invaded and took over operations.

Fascinated, Tank dug deeper. His search turned up 1890s-era German cartoons that featured the Yantarny Amber Mine. In one, miners stood knee-deep in gray water, pickaxes over their shoulders and their faces scrunched up against the stench of sulfur. Another showed heavily muscled men struggling to wrestle shoring timbers into place. A third depicted a long line of workers standing barefoot while uniformed officials searched their boots and coat pockets for pilfered amber.

Tank was still digging when a low beep indicated

an incoming message. Bookmarking his search, he switched to secure messaging. His pulse kicked up when he saw it was an update to the message Interpol had sent in response to his inquiry several days ago. Quickly, he skimmed the new information.

Their initial run had found no current open file on males with a scar above his left eye but a surveillance photo just in from the field revised their profile on a small-time thug with known ties to the Russian mafia. When Tank clicked on the attachment, a digitized photo painted across the screen. It had obviously been taken from some distance and was shot across a busy street. Rain came down in sheets and obscured the faces of most of the pedestrians not sheltered by umbrellas.

The high-powered camera lens had captured two men in fairly vivid detail, though. One had his face turned away and his shoulders bunched against the rain. The other was gesturing with one arm and was obviously speaking to his companion. He'd been silhouetted against a restaurant or shop window displaying tobacco products and gold Cyrillic lettering. The still-livid scar above his left eye showed in precise detail.

Tank zinged back a request for information on the Bulgarian's current whereabouts. He then forwarded the photo and list of known aliases to U.S. intelligence agencies with an urgent request to verify whether Scarface had made a trip to the States anytime in recent weeks.

He glanced at the clock and saw it was just past 1:00

p.m. Kaliningrad time. Rebel and Blade should be with Bauer's cousin now. Hopefully, he'd have something solid to send them by they time they finished the interview.

Chapter 9

Clara Bauer Soloff possessed a bent, arthritic body and a keen mind unclouded by time. Unfortunately, she also exhibited the inbred distrust of all Westerners that characterized most Soviets who'd grown to adulthood during the worst of the Cold War. The feelings had been mutual, of course. Americans' paranoia about all things Communist had found a rabid mouthpiece in Senator McCarthy and had dominated U.S./U.S.S.R. relations for decades.

Nor did it help that Ms. Soloff had lived through the horrific purges of the Stalin era, when millions of Soviets were rounded up on the mere suspicion of disloyalty to the party and disappeared into death camps. Tortured by the secret police, brothers had been forced to inform on brothers and sons on fathers. Given those historical perspectives, Rebel wasn't surprised Clara Soloff eyed them with a mix of curiosity and suspicion when a nurse wheeled her into the visitors' lounge.

The attendant shared her charge's reservations about Westerners. She braked the wheelchair and stood behind it, arms crossed, while Rebel introduced herself and Blade.

"My name is Victoria Talbot, Mrs. Soloff. This is my associate, Clint Black."

They'd debated whether to use a translator. During her assignment to Moscow Rebel had picked up all kinds of interesting tidbits from locals who didn't know she could understand them. But she'd suspected Mrs. Soloff might be reluctant to discuss an American cousin who'd operated behind the lines in front of others. If she would talk to them at all, that is.

"These are for you."

Hoping the woman wasn't diabetic, Rebel passed her the paper-wrapped bouquet and tin of chocolates they'd picked up at the hotel's gift shop. A sepia-toned picture of Königsberg Castle in its full glory decorated the tin's lid. Soloff thanked them for the gifts but her expression remained wary.

"Why do you come?"

"We just want to talk to you."

"Why? I'm an old woman. No one cares what an old woman has to say about anything."

"It's a personal matter. We would like to speak in private, if that's acceptable."

She considered that for some moments. Finally, curiosity overcame suspicion and she passed the flowers to the nurse. "Please put these in water for me, Galina."

"Are you sure, Clara?"

"I'm sure." She flapped a liver-spotted hand. "Go. Go."

The attendant squeaked off in her thick-soled Adidas. Rebel waited until she was out of earshot to begin with the opening she and Blade had decided to use.

"We're investigating the murder of an American woman."

"An American was killed here, in Kalinigrad?" Soloff shook her head. "The *Bratva* grows more vicious every day."

"She's talking about the Brotherhood," Rebel translated. "The Russian mafia."

"Those Georgians," the woman continued in disgust. "They and the Chechens and the Bulgarians sell drugs and guns on the streets. And the police—the *oblast*— they turn a blind eye. Half of them are in the pay of the gangs. No one is safe anymore."

"The woman I mentioned wasn't killed here," Rebel explained. "She was murdered in America. Her name was Vivian Bauer. She was the granddaughter of your cousin, Thomas Bauer."

Soloff looked blank for a moment. But only a moment. Rebel could tell the instant the name connected.

"Thomas's grandchild was killed?"

"Murdered."

"I'm sorry to hear that but…" She made a fluttery gesture with her hands. "I don't see what her death has to do with me."

"We think it may be connected to your cousin's activities during World War II."

The wariness came back, adding sharpness to her eyes and years to her lined face.

"Thomas's father and yours were brothers, weren't they?"

She darted a furtive glance at the desk and didn't reply.

Rebel tried again. "We're told your cousin's family emigrated to the United States when Kaliningrad was still the East Prussian province of Königsberg. Is that right, Mrs. Soloff?"

Still she remained silent. Rebel had almost given up hope of getting any information from her when Blade leaned forward to take one of the older woman's hands in his. His gaze held Clara's as he wrapped her in a cloak of quiet sincerity.

"Tell her we know her cousin came back to Königsberg in the last months of the war," he instructed Rebel. "If he contacted anyone in her family, they must have been terrified the Nazis would find out and execute them all. We understand why she wouldn't want to talk about his activities then. Or even after the war, when she said having a relative who'd trained as an American spy might cast doubt on her own loyalty as a Soviet citizen."

Clara never took her eyes off his. She didn't say anything, but as Rebel put his words into Russian she could see the older woman's misgivings melt by perceptible degrees. What was it about the man that got him past the barriers of any and all females? Rebel wondered ruefully.

Not that he'd slipped past hers last night. He'd bulldozed right through them. She had the whisker burns to prove it. She was surprised her butt didn't sport a few burns, too, given all the friction it and the wall had generated.

"We think there's a possibility her cousin may have stumbled on the missing Amber Room panels."

With a wrench, she resumed her translating duties.

"If so," Blade continued, "and she helps us find them, she'll be doing a great service to both Germany and to Russia."

It might have been the mention of the Amber Room that got her to talk. Or the calm voice that said she could trust this stranger who'd walked in off the street and asked her to share long-hidden secrets. Or the strong, sure hand that held hers. God knew his hands had elicited responses from Rebel she'd never imagined herself giving. Whatever the reason, Clara Bauer Soloff let her breath out on a rippling sigh.

"You have to understand how it was after the war. There was much hatred toward the Prussians. So much hatred. The Soviet Army executed many when they took the city. Then, just months later, the remaining citizens of Königsberg were given only hours to gather what they could carry and leave homes they had lived in all their lives. Soviet families who'd lost *their* homes in the war soon arrived by trainload."

A distant look came into her eyes while Rebel gave Blade the gist of what she'd said.

"My papa and mama and brother had died in the last days of the shelling," Soloff continued quietly. "When the order came down to leave, I was all alone. And I was pregnant. I had been raped, you see, and couldn't bear to go on. I tried to drown myself in the river."

She stared down at her hand with its papery, spotted skin and arthritic knuckles, still clasped in Blade's.

"Janik Soloff dragged me out. He was a good man, a private in the Red Army. He convinced me to marry him and bribed the authorities to let me stay. But the others, the ones who'd survived the air raids and the shelling and the hand-to-hand fighting, were forced to leave. Those few of us who remained never spoke of our German roots."

She lifted her gaze to her visitors.

"It was not safe, you understand. After the war, during the purges that followed, even today."

"I understand," Rebel said. "But you don't need to be afraid to talk to us. Whatever you tell us will remain in strictest confidence."

"Do you think so?" Her voice took on a dry note. "Then you do not know the FSB."

She eased her hand from Blade's. Rebel thought that might be the end of their discussion but Soloff surprised her by returning to the reason for their visit.

"I saw Thomas only once during the war. I didn't recognize him at first. None of us did. He showed up at our door covered in gray dust, carrying a pickax on his shoulder like one of the miners from Yarntany."

Blade caught the name and shot Rebel a swift look. She translated quickly before prompting Clara to continue.

"Thomas came to see my papa. To ask him about the tunnels."

"What tunnels?"

"Those beneath the castle." She traced a fingertip over the design on the tin of chocolates. "Thomas had a map. His papa had drawn it for him. But with the air raids and constant shelling, many buildings had collapsed and whole streets were obliterated. Thomas could no longer make any sense of his map."

"Did your father help him decipher it?"

Her finger stilled. Even after so many years, the terror and uncertainty of those last months of the war echoed in her stark account.

"We all knew the end was near. The bombs rained down like fire from the sky. The Russians—my own Janik among them—were advancing. My papa was a loyal Prussian but he thought… He hoped…" She drew in a quivering breath. "Thomas promised he would tell his superiors in the American Army that papa aided him. See that our family was taken care of. But my parents and brother died and then, after the Russians took the city, I married Janik. There was no one left for Thomas to take care of."

"You didn't see him again after that one night?"

"No."

"Even after the war? He didn't come back? Or try to contact you?"

"There was one letter. It was addressed to my papa and had been routed through several refugee camps in Germany. It took two years to come into my hands."

"Do you remember what it said?"

"Only that Thomas had asked Red Cross officials to search for us and, if this letter found us, we were to contact him."

"Did you?"

"No. I had my husband and my baby. And with the purges still going on…"

She left it at that. Disappointed, Rebel tried a different tack.

"My friend mentioned the Amber Room. Did you see it when it was on display here in Königsberg?"

"Of course. Such a magnificent work of art. Everyone was so thrilled to have it back in Prussia, where it was first crafted. Papa took us to see it," she recalled with a misty smile. "Mama and my brother and me. We walked up to the castle. It was Saturday. Saturday afternoon. Sunny and bright and still early in the war, so there were no ruins or bomb craters to hinder us. Afterward, we ate *klopse* at mama's favorite restaurant."

"Do you remember if your cousin said anything about the amber panels the night he came to your house?"

She shook her head. "He didn't. I'm sure he didn't. I would have remembered…"

"Clara?" The rubbery squeak of sneakers preceded the nurse's return. "You shouldn't tire yourself like this." She directed the comment to the woman in the wheelchair but made sure the visitors got the message. "Shall I take you back to your room?"

"In a minute, Galina." She held up an arthritic hand. "My cousin didn't mention the Amber Room. I'm sure of that. But I think… He said something…" Her face screwed into a frown. "Something about the mine reclaiming its treasures."

The mine again! Rebel was becoming more and more convinced the answer to the puzzle lay somewhere in its murky depths. She didn't look forward to another close encounter of the bat variety but couldn't see any way out of it.

Blade confirmed her glum supposition after they'd thanked Clara Soloff and said goodbye. The sun burned in a bright blue sky and their hotel was within walking distance, so they decided to hoof it.

"We can stop on the way and pick up some high-powered flashlights. Better change, too, before we tackle that abandoned tunnel."

They would have to face the tunnel sooner rather than later, but Rebel yielded to the craven impulse to put it off a little longer. "Maybe we should check out the museum first. I bet it'll have information on mine operations."

"Fine by me. You remember how to get there?"

"It was part of the old city walls. We'll have to cross the river and head back toward the House of Soviets." Smiling, she quoted their cab driver. "The ugliest building in all Russia."

She could see it across the river. The square, blue-painted concrete tower provided a sad contrast to the stained-glass windows and ornate red brick of Kaliningrad's lovingly restored cathedral. The cathedral's conical steeples rose above the shimmery, lime-green lindens and provided a clearly visible landmark.

They kept it in their line of sight as they passed the shops lining this side of the river. The goods in store windows gave fascinating glimpses into Kaliningrad's past. Amber was everywhere. In fine jewelry, in furniture, in cheap souvenirs. One shop proudly displayed a whole selection of Elvis amber products. Key chains, statuettes, even imitation vinyl records with his song labels picked out in bits of yellow.

Antique shops offered a wealth of insight into the city's long and often turbulent history. Prussian helmets topped with iron spikes or sweeping horsetails sat side-by-side with military memorabilia inscribed with red swastikas. Dented brass samovars vied for space with mismatched pieces of Meissen china. A set of military beer steins marched across one window, each topped with incredibly detailed infantry or cavalry figures.

Fascinated by the displays, Rebel almost missed the sign pointing to another shop tucked at the back of a narrow alley.

"Hey! We should check out this shop. They specialize in antique maps. Bet they have some of Königsberg before the war."

They did, but none that depicted the tunnels under the castle or the city's sewer system. The proprietor was a squat, bald stump of a man who didn't try to hide his amusement at their request.

"You look for the Amber Room, yes?"

"Well…"

"You would not be the first," he said, chuckling. "So many have searched. I supplied city maps to the Soviet Commission who dug through the rubble of the castle one final time before it was bulldozed to build the House of Soviets. And to the professor who came five years ago, sure she had found a clue in some musty letter she had discovered. Even today they hunt. Germans, Russians, British, Bulgarians. Now you Americans."

Rebel took a stab. "Has anyone besides us been in lately? Within the past two or three weeks?"

"No. Although someone calls yesterday. I tell him what I tell you. The Amber Room panels no longer exist. They were destroyed in the war, along with almost seventy percent of this city."

The visit to the museum proved just as disappointing.

Rebel learned more than she would have ever imagined possible about the myths, legends and history of amber. She also read every detail describing the Amber Room's brief return to its Prussian origins during WWII. She studied the black-and-white photos of the room's exposition in Königsberg Castle. She spoke at length to the museum's curator. But when she and Blade departed the museum, they were no closer to knowing if Thomas Bauer had stumbled on the missing panels than when they'd gone in.

"Today's been a total loss so far," she commented as they headed for their hotel.

"You think so, huh?"

She caught his crooked grin. "Oh. Well. The morning wasn't so bad. Pretty damned good, as a matter of fact. Here, we can cut through this alley. It should take us to the street our hotel's on."

Unlike the alley housing the map shop, this one contained no stores or display windows. The cobbled path was narrow and dark and smelled faintly of urine. Brick walls covered with graffiti leaned in on both sides. Most of the scrawled messages were just obscene, although one or two aspired to pornographic poetry.

She was more than happy to see the busy, sunlit sidewalk dead ahead. As they emerged, Blade's phone emitted a distinctive signal. She glanced over her shoulder, saw him slide it out of his pocket.

"Yo, Tank."

He walked toward her, the phone to his ear, and Rebel swung back around just in time to avoid a collision with two men on the outer sidewalk.

"Excuse me," she said in Russian. "I didn't..."

"You!"

The curse exploded from a face twisted with disbelief. The same face she'd glimpsed through the pouring rain yesterday, she realized as her breath got stuck in her throat. It lodged there like an ice cube swallowed unintentionally, freezing her from the inside out, as she took in the jagged scar the face had acquired since the last time they'd come nose to nose.

Feodyr Chernak. Or whatever alias the slime was going by now.

With another curse, the Bulgarian shot out a hand and stiff-armed her back into the alley. The violent move knocked Rebel into Blade and sent his comm device flying. The phone hit the brick wall, dropped to the cobbles, was still clattering when Chernak spun out a lethal little Marakov 9mm.

"Bitch," he snarled in his gutter Russian. "They told me you were dead."

Blade reacted so swiftly his movements were a blur in the dim alleyway. Shoving Rebel aside with one hand, he delivered a bone-shattering chop to Chernak's wrist with the other. He was reaching for the Sig nested in its ankle holster when Rebel realized she had only seconds to act.

She tore at the flap of her purse. Closed her fist around her .38. Whipped it up and shoved the barrel into the back of Blade's neck.

"Drop it."

"What the hell…!"

"Drop it," she repeated icily, "or I'll take a page from our friend here and blow a nice, neat hole in your throat."

Chapter 10

Sheer surprise froze the three men in place as Rebel gouged her gun barrel deeper into Blade's neck and repeated her icy command.

"Drop it. Now."

He lowered his arm, slowly, and let the Sig clatter to the cobbles.

"Smart move."

Pulling her lips back in a feral smile, she addressed the man she'd last encountered at what was supposed to have been a deserted airstrip on the outskirts of Moscow.

"So, Feodyr. You thought I was dead, did you? Lucky for you I'm very much alive."

"But..." He stared at her with slitted eyes and

wrapped his free hand around the wrist Blade must have come near to shattering with that vicious chop. "I saw Karinski lunge for you! I saw the blood when you hit the dirt."

"It wasn't my blood, as you would have discovered if you'd stuck around until the shooting stopped." She shifted her attention to the second man. "You! Pick up this one's gun."

He looked to his partner for direction. Chernak gave a jerky nod. When he'd retrieved Blade's weapon, she issued another curt order.

"He's got a knife strapped to his right arm. Get it. Carefully!"

She was speaking Russian. Blade didn't understand a word. But she felt his already wire-tight muscles tense even more when Chernak's partner took a step toward him.

"Don't move," she warned in English. "Do not move."

She was still standing behind him, her weapon dug into his skin, and didn't pull in a breath until Chernak's partner stepped back with the bone knife in hand. She relieved the pressure on Blade's neck but kept the .38 leveled on his head as she backed up a few paces.

"What is this?" Chernak snarled, still holding his wrist. "Why are you in Kaliningrad?"

"The same reason you are, Feodyr. Or are you using another alias? You have so many, I've lost count."

He ignored the name issue, as she'd expected he

would, and spit out a demand. "Tell me. Why are you here?"

"I'm searching for the Amber Room. Like you."

"How do you know this?"

"You're too sloppy, Feodyr. You left the Bauer woman alive. She died in my arms, but not before she choked out a description. I didn't put it together until just now, though. The scar threw me. You didn't have it when you turned tail and ran in Moscow."

His thin, handsome face flushed almost as red as the barely healed wound above his eye but he didn't dispute her account of that memorable night. Mainly because he couldn't.

"And this one?" He jerked his chin at Blade. "Who is he, and why do you now keep him at gunpoint?"

"I wouldn't have to if you hadn't announced to the whole friggin' world that you knew me. Christ! I hate having to deal with amateurs."

"But…"

"You want to stand here all day reminiscing?" she interrupted impatiently. "Or shall we take this conversation some place a little more private?"

Red surged into his face again. He didn't like taking orders from a woman. Especially one who'd treated him with such amused contempt the last time they'd collaborated.

"We have a place," he ground out. "One block from here."

"Let's go."

When he hesitated, his cheeks still suffused with red, Rebel merely lifted a brow.

"All right, all right. But first…"

He edged past Blade and bent to retrieve his 9 mm. When he straightened, he came in from behind and swung his arm in a vicious arc. The Marakov's butt smashed into Blade's temple.

Grunting, he staggered forward. Blade caught himself after another half step and pivoted, his fists bunched and murder in his eyes. Chernak slapped his hand on the slide and cocked the Marakov with a snap that ricocheted off the brick walls like a rifle shot.

"Go ahead," Rebel drawled. "Shoot him. You've mangled this business so badly already you might as well silence the only person who can get to the amber panels."

Chernak's nostrils flared. A vein bulged in his forehead, mere inches from the still healing scar. The urge to kill was written all across his face until she ended the showdown with a huff of disgust.

"For God's sake, you've proved you're a man! Now tuck your penis back into your shorts and let's get moving before someone stops to see what all the commotion is about."

He sent her an evil look but gestured to his companion to move out of the alley. "You go first, Nikolai. Then you and your friend, Viktoria. I'll walk behind to make sure we all arrive safely."

"Whatever." She switched to English and met Blade's

stone-cold stare. "These nice gentlemen have invited us up to their place. Just follow Nikolai here."

She could see him searching for some clue to what was going down in her face, her eyes. She kept both carefully bland as she slid the snub nosed .38 into her purse. She left her hand in the open purse, her finger curled around the trigger, and gestured to Nikolai.

"Let's go."

Her comm device vibrated before they'd taken more than a couple steps. One long shimmy, two short. OMEGA control's silent, urgent demand for verification of status. She couldn't answer verbally. Not with Chernak hard on her heels. But she could send a coded signal. She pressed three digits, then flicked a switch to mute the phone.

"Okay," she said to Blade. "Let's move it."

He did, his head hurting like a son of a bitch with every step. The pain hammered at him with unrelenting force as he tried to make sense of the past five minutes.

What in hell was Rebel up to? She obviously knew this Feodyr asshole. Blade had to assume they'd crossed paths in her other life. She must have tagged the man as Vivian Bauer's killer. The scar was a dead giveaway. So why was she playing along with him? She had to have a good reason, but it pissed Blade no end that she hadn't tried to communicate by so much as a blink or a muscle twitch back there in the alley.

That reminded him of the "urgent" flash on his comm device. Tank had just been about to explain the signal when Rebel had sent the damned device flying out of Blade's hands. It was still in the alley, right alongside his manhood. Christ! He couldn't remember the last time he'd let someone get the drop on him. Of course, he hadn't expected that someone to be his partner.

Head hammering, he swung between going along with whatever scheme Rebel had hatched and taking these two thugs out. He could do it now that he had their measure. Alone if necessary, although it would be easier if his partner had given him some damn clue what was going down.

That brought him back full circle. Frustrated, he gave up trying to decipher her game plan. Easier to sketch a mental profile of these two characters for identification purposes later. Nikolai was five-nine or -ten. Swarthy complexion. Dark hair, brown eyes, faded jeans, new Reeboks, a Breitling Airwolf chronometer strapped to his wrist. The watch would've cost two or three thousand U.S. if he'd bought it, which Blade considered highly unlikely.

His pal was taller, lighter complexioned and more dangerous. The kind who killed for pleasure as well as business. Blade had run across a few like Feodyr over the years. He hoped to hell Rebel had a handle on the man or they both might end up in the river he could see some distance ahead.

He used that ribbon of gray and the cathedral's tall spire as reference points to fix their location in his mind. They were still on a main boulevard but soon left it to turn onto first one narrow side street, then another. With each turn the shops and apartments grew progressively less enticing. Some moments later Nikolai halted in front of a narrow wooden door with peeling blue paint. He jiggled an old fashioned brass latch but had to add a swift kick before the door opened onto a dark, dank entryway.

The mingled odors of old cooking grease and new sweat smacked Blade in the face as he followed Nikolai up two flights of stairs and down a narrow hall. Their footsteps thudded on cracked linoleum flooring. Water leaks stained the walls. This dump didn't go with the Airwolf that Nikolai sported, unless these were temporary quarters he and his pal had decided to squat in while they hunted for plundered treasure.

Nikolai knuckled a coded signal on the door at the end of the hall. Two quick raps, a pause, another rap. A chain rattled, locks clicked, and a hairy ape in a sweat-stained undershirt materialized. He stood aside, raking both Blade and Rebel with a surprised look as they marched in and fired off what sounded like the Russian version of "What the hell?"

Since Blade couldn't understand the terse explanations that followed, he used the interval to scope out the dingy apartment. The main room contained a beat-up chrome-legged table fronted by three cheap plastic chairs and a stained sofa planted in front of a sixty-two-inch flat-screen TV that had probably been lifted off the back end of a delivery truck. The kitchen was a sink, a hot plate, a fridge and some open-shelved cupboards.

Two bedrooms opened off the main room, both with unmade beds and mismatched furniture. A female wearing pink panties and a midriff-baring black T-shirt sat slumped on the edge of one bed. She was probably in her late teens or early twenties. Hard to tell given her dull, wasted eyes and the bruises purpling one side of her face.

"You! Sit there."

The barked command came from the one Rebel had called Feodyr. He emphasized his point by jabbing the muzzle of his Marakov toward one of the plastic chairs. Blade ignored both the command and the jab.

"So you speak English."

"When I wish," the blond sneered. "Not everyone is like you Americans, too lazy or too ignorant to learn any language but your own. Sit, and I will have Viktoria explain why I should not shoot you between the eyes and dump your body in the river."

Rebel showed no reaction to the threat. Other than a moue of disgust as she glanced around the squalid apartment, she'd registered no emotion at all. She'd better have something good up her sleeve, Blade thought grimly as he folded his frame into the chair. Damned good!

Feodyr issued another command, in Russian this time. Apeman gave him a sour look but humped into one of the bedrooms. When he reappeared a few moments later with handcuffs dangling from a meaty fist, Blade conducted another fierce internal debate. Every instinct he possessed resisted the idea of voluntary restraint. What's more, he fully intended to pay Blondie back for that smack on the head by kicking his ass from here to Sunday.

He had to balance instinct and intent against Rebel's game, though. Whatever the hell that game was. Once again his eyes cut to hers. Once again she gave no clue. Jaw locked, Blade let Apeman yank his arms behind his back. The bastard ratcheted the cuffs on so tight they bit almost to the bone.

He could get out of them if he had to. It would take some doing, but he could inch his belt through the waistband loops on his jeans, get it to his back. The buckle's metal tongue was flat and strong enough to use as a shim. He should know. He'd honed it himself. Granted not with this purpose in mind, but Blade had found more than one use for a sharp, pointy object in the past.

What he didn't know were the parameters of this dangerous game Rebel was playing. Thoroughly pissed at being left to flounder around in the dark, he flexed his wrists to keep the blood flowing.

"Now we talk, Viktoria."

Rebel's heart was slamming against her ribs and a flophouse sweat trickled between her breasts, but she merely lifted a brow as Chernak yanked out a second plastic chair and kicked it across the scarred linoleum.

He claimed the third, dropped into it, and rested his arm on the tabletop with the Marakov within easy reach.

She tried to remember where in Bulgaria he was from. Not Sofia, the capital. Somewhere farther east, closer to the Black Sea. Balchik, she thought, although he'd spent so many years dealing drugs and guns and prostitutes on the streets of Moscow he could probably qualify as a native.

"Who is this guy?" he asked, reverting to his heavily accented Russian.

"His name is Clint Black."

She didn't glance at Blade. Couldn't. If looks were bone-handled knives, she would be feeling a dozen stab wounds by now.

"He's a treasure hunter," she said coolly. "Like you."

"How do you come to be with him?"

Suspicion coated Chernak's every syllable. With good reason. The last time she'd come face-to-face to him the world had pretty much blown up in their faces.

As Major Victoria Talbot, she'd squeezed her air force connections to arrange transport of a planeload of unprocessed opium from Afghanistan. The Russian mafia's second in command had driven out to oversee the hand-off personally. Karinski had gone down in the blaze of gunfire that lit up the night. She could still hear the bullets thudding into the body that slammed into hers and took them both to the tarmac.

"Things got a little too hot for me after that mess in

Moscow," she said with a careless shrug. "I decided it was best all around if I left the military."

"I always wondered about that." His chair tipped on its rear legs, he studied her intently through the screen of his pale lashes. "How you could wear the uniform of the United States and yet have so many contacts with the *bratva?*"

This was getting too close to a swirling vortex of lies and deceit that might well suck her in. Rebel had to tread carefully here. Very carefully.

"I found the brotherhood useful."

"You, or your government? Or," he said slowly, watching her closely, "were you working both sides? Like—how do you call it? The…uh…" He fumbled until he finally found the words he wanted in English. "Double agent?"

The vortex swirled faster and angrier by the second. Rebel didn't so much as glance at Blade, but she almost could feel him icing over.

"It doesn't matter what I was or wasn't. As I said, things got too hot for me after Moscow. Now I free-lance."

"Freelance? What is this?"

"I work for myself."

The Bulgarian looked less than convinced. "You hire yourself out to treasure hunters, as you say that one is?"

"Why not?" Her eyes were cool, her smile satirical. "C'mon, Feodyr. You know as well as I do the missing Amber Room panels are worth a thousand times more than what we would have pulled in from that botched opium deal. You wouldn't have flown to the States and hunted down Vivian Bauer otherwise."

She didn't look at Blade to see how he'd reacted to her mention of the Amber Room and Vivian Bauer. She didn't dare.

"Did the Bauer woman give you anything useful before you shot her?" she asked Chernak. "Or Kurov, before you or your pal here threw him out the window?"

"Why should I tell you?"

When he didn't bother to deny he'd had a hand in either death, rage knotted Rebel's belly. Savagely, she repressed it. She couldn't lose her cool with Chernak. He was a minor slug in the Russian mafia hierarchy, but given half a chance he would eat her alive.

"You should tell me because we've both landed here in Kaliningrad. Whatever you learned from your sources got you this far. Same with me. Where we go from here is the question."

"You think so?" Chernak tipped his chair onto its rear legs again. "If, as you say, you have useful information regarding the amber panels, there are ways to extract it. Drugs. Knives. Or, as my friend Nikolai here particularly enjoys, clamping electrodes to nipples and testicles."

"Electrodes really worked for you back in Moscow, didn't they?" Her smile turned biting. "If the information you extracted from your so-called informant hadn't been so garbled by torture, we might not have been caught in a cross fire. Incidentally, how did you explain that little foul-up to your bosses?"

Red surged into his cheeks, fury into his eyes. Rebel noted both with vicious satisfaction.

"So you couldn't explain it, huh?" Her lip curling, she let her glance circle the room. "Must be why you're operating out of such a dump."

She thought he might lose it then. The angry red had reached all the way to his hairline. Not a real good color for him. She decided she'd probably stomped on his ego hard enough and throttled back on the sneer.

"My guess is that you're still trying to recover from that fiasco. Show your bosses you can score something big. I can help you."

He drummed his fingers on the cracked table, thinking, considering, weighing. "If we make this score," he said at last, "what percentage do you think to take from it?"

"We split any profits fifty-fifty."

It was his turn to curl a lip. "You're in Russian territory, Viktoria, searching for Russian artifacts long sought by the central government. You couldn't get whatever you found—if you found anything—out of Kaliningrad without someone who knows which custom inspectors to bribe, which border guards are corrupt."

"That would be true—if I was planning to go through customs or cross borders."

Chernak didn't quite succeed in hiding his sudden interest. "You have an alternate plan?"

"I always have an alternate plan." Rebel let that sink in for a few moments before pushing out of her chair with a show of impatience. "Look, we both know you don't have the authority to make this kind of a deal. Talk to whoever you're working for these days. Tell him how close you are—or aren't—to finding the amber panels. Then we'll settle on percentages." She rotated her neck to relieve the tension, both real and pretended. "In the meantime, I'll take my friend in the other room and explain the situation. Let me know when you're ready to close the deal."

"Wait." Chernak surged to his feet and planted himself in her path. "Nikolai relieved your friend of his weapons. You won't mind if I do the same for you."

"Don't you trust me?"

"No."

She show her teeth in a nasty smile. "You're finally wising up a little."

Since he already had his hand on her purse strap, she surrendered it without a fight. He tossed it on the table and turned back to her with an equally nasty smile. Rebel rolled her eyes when he palmed her breasts but let him run his hands down her hips and legs to her ankles. When he started back up and aimed for her crotch, she'd had enough.

"Slide those hands any higher and you'll be eating your nuts for supper."

For the first time since they'd collided outside the

alley, Chernak relaxed enough to laugh. Straightening, he hooked his thumbs in his belt.

"That's what I like about American women. They usually put up a good fight. Not like that sorry excuse for a whore in the other room."

Rebel's rage flared white-hot again. Savagely, she tamped it down to only a barb. "Judging by the bruises on her face, I'd say she put up a pretty good fight. How old is she, Feodyr? Nineteen? Twenty?"

"Why do you care?"

She shouldn't. She'd been activated for a mission that could significantly impact U.S.-Russian relations. She would have to answer for her actions to Lightning, maybe to the President of the United States. Yet she couldn't ignore either the vicious bruising or the hopeless slump to the girl's shoulders.

"How old is she?"

Chernak turned to the thug with the overabundance of body hair and sweat-stained armpits. "She's your toy, Anatoli. Do you know her age?"

"No." He scratched his chest. "She was snatched from a schoolyard. That much I do know. Still a virgin when they brought her here. But the sale fell through, so I decided to keep her to amuse me and my friends."

Chernak turned back with a look on his face that said he could care less where the girl had come from or what happened to her after he and his pals were finished with her. Most likely, Rebel guessed with another spurt of rage, she would end up in the river.

"Call your boss," she told Cherak with no effort to hide her disgust. "We'll talk again when you're serious about negotiating." Switching to English, she crooked a finger at Blade. "Come with me."

Great, she fumed as she led the way. Just great! Now she had a kidnapped schoolgirl to worry about in addition to a homicidal Bulgarian, a presidential directive and a long-lost national treasure.

When she passed the room where the teenager sat slumped on the end of the bed, Rebel wanted to signal a message, send her a tiny spark of hope, but the girl looked at the newcomers with dilated, unfocused pupils that registered nothing but a dull despair.

Jaw tight, Rebel stopped just inside the second bedroom. Chernak and his friend couldn't have occupied it for more than a few days but they'd left their mark in empty vodka bottles and unwashed clothes. She lowered herself onto the edge of the mattress, sincerely hoping the dingy gray sheets weren't infested with bedbugs. Or worse.

She expected Blade to be pissed. She also expected him to demand an explanation. She couldn't give him one. Not with these paper-thin walls and three goons only a whisper away. He would just have to trust her.

But when she hissed that to him, he positioned himself so he blocked the view from the other rooms. Rebel wasn't sure how a handcuffed man could look and feel so threatening, but a ridiculous shiver rippled along her spine when he echoed two soft, dangerous words.

"Double agent?"

Chapter 11

Nick Jensen parked his Jag and keyed the private entrance to his office. It wasn't quite 8:00 a.m. Chelsea shouldn't have been in yet, but of course she was. He'd given up reminding her that the agents on duty in the Control Center would contact him anytime day or night of significant activity affecting operatives in the field. They also had standing orders to provide an update as soon as he arrived each morning. Chelsea insisted on making sure that happened smoothly and efficiently.

Nick had never thought anyone could replace the woman who'd served as the Special Envoy's executive assistant for more than a decade. Like every other OMEGA agent he'd fallen completely under the spell of Elizabeth Wells. He'd been as smitten by the silver-haired grandmother's smiling warmth as by the fact she could dead center four out of five rounds. He'd still acutely missed Elizabeth when he'd hired Chelsea Jackson.

Warmth wasn't one of Chelsea's shining attributes, Nick thought as she responded to the silent signal triggered with the key. She exuded an air of cool reserve that belied the dark fire in her hair. Which was probably why she'd succeeded so well at the variety of jobs she'd held while putting herself through high school and college. Including the job that Nick flatly refused to let himself think about while she greeted him with a polite smile.

"Good morning, sir."

"Morning, Chelsea."

"Dodge and Tank called down a few minutes ago," she informed him as she aligned three color-coded files on his desk. "They're standing by for the morning brief. Shall I have them come down?"

"No, I'll go up."

Since he hadn't received a flash from either agent, he wasn't expecting to find them with their heads together and each wearing a frown. A familiar itch started just under Lightning's skin. He'd been in this job too long, he decided as the itch raced along his nerves like an out-of-control bush fire. One look at a controller's body language, and he was already fearing the worst.

His glance flew instinctively to the status board with the map showing the location of field operatives.

The absence of flashing red lights confirmed none was down. Relieved, Lightning snagged a cup of coffee before joining the two controllers.

"What's up?"

Since Tank was the newbie and still showing his stuff, Dodge let him take the lead. "We're not sure. I was in the middle of relaying information to Blade when his comm device went dead."

Lightning bit back an instant rebuttal. His wife had designed OMEGA's communicators. They were water-, fire-, earthquake- and bombproof. Mackenzie claimed the only thing that might knock one out was a direct hit from a fiery meteor tearing through the earth's atmosphere to hit at twenty or thirty thousand miles per hour. To her intense disappointment she'd never had an opportunity to put that hypothesis to the test.

Thankfully, Tank spared Lightning the task of informing his wife one of her babies had failed by amending his first statement. "Well, it's not actually dead. It's still sending a signal. We tracked it to a back alley in Kaliningrad. Blade's last transmission has us a little worried, though."

He played a recording of the brief voice communication. It opened with "Yo, Tank" and terminated mere seconds later with "What the hell…?" That was followed by the clatter of the phone smashing into something solid and several indistinct voices.

"Jane amplified the soundtrack and analyzed the voiceprints."

With a nod to the communications technician who'd worked some acoustical magic, Tank slid up the volume control. Even without Jane O'Conner's verification Lightning had no trouble identifying Rebel as the one issuing the icy command to "drop it." Most of the terse dialogue that followed was in Russian, translated by Dodge.

Lightning listened intently. His brows soared at Rebel's sarcastic suggestion to someone to shoot Blade but he said nothing until she ordered her partner to follow some character named Nikolai.

"Did you get a fix on the people she's talking to?"

"We think we know one of them," Tank confirmed.

Tersely, he briefed Lightning on the information he'd received on the Bulgarian thug known variously as Kiril Deniv, Bogdan Chornasemski and Feodyr Chernak.

"I had just started to relay the information to Blade when our transmission was interrupted."

"Did you get the ID to Rebel?"

"I tried. I sent a request for status verification first. She came back with a five-four-eight."

Situation under control, going no-comm.

The first part of the coded signal Lightning accepted. The analysis of Rebel's voiceprint had detected surprise and a sharp spike in tension but no panic. Whatever was going on over there, she obviously felt confident she could handle it. The second part bothered him. Operatives didn't cut themselves off from their safety net except in extraordinary circumstances.

He had to respect her situational assessment, though. She was the agent on scene. One of them, anyway.

"What's their current location?"

Tank brought up a digital map and zeroed in on a block of run-down apartments. The imagery was so precise Lightning could see a pot of tired-looking geraniums in the window of one apartment and wash strung out to dry on the rusted iron balcony of another. A beeping light indicated the signal emanating from a third-floor apartment at the north end of the building.

"Notify our contact in Moscow to stand by. Tell him we might need assistance in Kaliningrad. And I want you on the next plane to the Baltic," he instructed Dodge.

Tank didn't protest being left out of the action, although both men could see the effort it required. Dodge gave his upper arm a sympathetic punch that rocked him back a step.

"You've got the next one. Assuming you make it through Offensive Tactics, of course."

"I'll make it."

"Hope so. Better men than you and I have crawled home, bawling for their mommas. In the meantime, watch my back."

"Will do."

"And contact me as soon as either Rebel or Blade reopen their comm link. Sure would be nice to know what in blazes is going on with them."

Double agent.

The phrase looped repeatedly in Blade's mind as he

tried to find a comfortable position on the lumpy mattress. The whispered command from Rebel a half hour ago hadn't broken the vicious cycle. Trust her. That's the only bone she'd tossed him. He was supposed to trust her. Like he had a choice?

Now she was in the other room, summoned by Scarface to continue a discussion Blade had been cut out of. Seething, he listened to the rise and fall of their voices. They were speaking Russian, which irritated him even more since he now knew Chernak had a working knowledge of English. Rebel could have found a way to switch. Give Blade some clue to what they were talking about. The question of why she hadn't kickstarted the loop again.

Double agent.

She couldn't be! Everything in him repudiated the idea. They'd had their differences, sure. The woman had been in his face since the hour she'd arrived at OMEGA. But there was no way in hell a military academy grad turned air force pilot turned OMEGA operative could have passed so many background checks without some hint of an alter ego turning up.

Riiiight, a stubborn corner of his mind sneered. *Just like she couldn't toss you on your ass. Or spark a hunger so fierce you'd damned near wrung yourself inside out making love to her.*

No! She'd been right there with him. Blade was sure of that. She couldn't have faked that panting urgency or those back-arching, throat-closing, mind-blowing climaxes.

Riiiight.

Dammit it all to hell! He was sick of the doubts. Tired of not knowing which side of Victoria Talbot was real and which was a role she'd played in her shadowy past. Or, that same insidious corner of his mind jeered, maybe he just refused to admit they might be one and the same.

He knew one thing for certain. This was the last time he would play dumbass and let some goon like Apeman restrain him. He'd be the one slapping on the cuffs on next time. And a certain tawny-haired operative wouldn't get out of them anytime soon. Nursing that dead certainty, he began inching his belt through the loops and around his waist.

"So, Viktoria. We are agreed?"

Rebel swallowed the foul taste in her mouth and nodded. After fifteen minutes of point/counterpoint, she and Chernak had negotiated a deal each knew the other had no intention of honoring.

"We are."

Chernak shot a quick glance at his cohorts. Nikolai and Hairy Harry occupied either end of the sagging sofa. They'd followed the negotiations with varying degrees of interest. Nikolai now looked impatient, Fur Ball mostly bored.

The girl hadn't moved or said a word this whole time. She still sat on the edge of the bed, shoulders hunched, face dull. These slimes would pay for that hopeless despair, Rebel vowed fiercely.

Blade had stretched out on the bed in the second bedroom. All she could see of him were his feet. Probably just as well. He'd made his displeasure at the situation crystal clear. He would like what might follow even less.

"All right, Viktoria. What do you know of the missing amber panels that we do not?"

"I know a number of people believe the statement of the one eyewitness who claims to have seen them crated, moved from Königsberg Castle and loaded onto a train in the last, frantic days before the Red Army arrived."

"Kurov told you this, yes?"

She neither confirmed nor denied the aged curator had been her source, but her bland look managed to convince Chernak that's why she'd traveled to Kaliningrad. She wasn't about to reveal Sergeant Thomas Bauer had worked for the OSS and been dropped behind enemy lines, right here in his old home town. And she sure as hell wasn't going to turn Feodyr and company loose on Clara Bauer Soloff.

"Kurov told us about this train, too," Chernak said dismissively. "But he could not say where it went from Königsberg Castle."

"So you shoved him out the window of his flat?"

Shrugging, he brushed the curator's death aside as totally irrelevant. "The old man was of no more use to us."

Rebel's sardonic smile made him realize he'd just put his foot in it. His handsome face turned smarmy and placating.

"We won't shove you out a window once you're no longer of use to us, Viktoria. You or your friend."

"No, you won't." Her voice was every bit as smarmy as his. "Because you need my friend to interpret the specs we've requested and you need me to convince him to do it."

Chernak dropped the Mr. Nice Guy facade. "What specs?"

"Give me my purse and I'll show you."

Suspicion flaring, he debated for several moments before issuing a gruff order. Nikolai heaved himself off the sofa, hooked the bag by its shoulder strap, ambled over and dropped it on the table. Chernak made a show of removing the snub-nosed .38 before sliding the purse across the chipped Formica.

With another cynical smile, Rebel extracted her comm device. A single glance confirmed her five-four-eight had been transmitted and received. OMEGA wouldn't contact her—or expect to hear from her—until she reversed the signal. She knew they were tracking her through the phone's GPS signal, though. She didn't doubt for a moment that Tank had her pinpointed on one of the Control Center's megascreens.

She used a thumb to scroll through the entries until she found an earlier message Tank had forwarded before all the nasty stuff started. Her heart thumping, she brought up the schematic of the entire Yantarny Mine system.

Bless him! He'd come through for them! She didn't have time for more than a skim of the drawing. She couldn't risk Chernak getting a glimpse of it. Hitting a scramble key, she turned the schematic into indecipherable lines of code before angling the phone toward the Bulgarian.

"Here they are."

He leaned forward eagerly but the anticipation sharpening his face morphed instantly into a scowl. "These are the specs you spoke of? I can't read them."

"Neither can I," Rebel replied with a touch of acid. "They're in HTML. Hypertext Markup Language."

"I know what HTML is," he fired back. "They use it on webpages."

"Exactly. So we'll need a computer to translate the HTML and my friend in the other room to interpret the specs once they're up."

"Interpret what?" Frustration and suspicion gave a sharp edge to the question. "What are these supposed specs for?"

"The Yantarny Mine."

"Yantarny? Where is this Yantarny?"

"Twenty five kilometers from Kaliningrad," Hairy Harry interjected. "On the Baltic." He scratched the matted black fur above his stained undershirt. "In the old days they brought raw amber from the mine to Königsberg Castle for sorting and grading."

"Brought it how?"

"Ox carts, in the time of the Teutonic knights. Trains later. Then the tunnels collapsed and they used trucks up until the mine shut down."

Rebel saw when the light dawned. It was like a strobe flashing in Chernak's eyes.

"Tunnels," he echoed, knifing her with a hard look. "These specs of yours. Do they show tunnels?"

"I don't know. We were on our way to an internet cafe when we were so rudely interrupted."

More or less. Rebel was giving herself high marks for inventiveness when Chernak sprang to his feet.

"I know where there's a laptop. You can transfer the file with a USB cord, can't you?"

She nodded, thrilled that he'd taken the bait.

"Nikolai! Get the other American. We can use Anatoli's car and…"

Rebel whipped up a hand. "Hold on, pal. You're forgetting your side of this deal. I've shown you what I bring to the table. Let's see what you've got."

He hesitated, and she could almost hear the wheels whirring again. Shaking her head, she jammed a spoke in the cogs.

"It won't do you any good to take the phone away from me and download the HTML file. You won't be able to read the schematic. I told you, you need Clint Black for that." When he still hesitated, she flapped an impatient hand. "Why the hell do you think I've nursed him along this far? Now pull your head out of your ass and show me what you've got."

He flushed but reached into his back pocket and produced a much creased document of some sort. Slapping it down on the table, he unfolded it to show what looked like an aerial map.

"This was taken by Soviet reconnaissance planes two weeks before the Red Army reached the outskirts of Königsberg." He gave her a smug smile. "A former counterpart of yours in the Russian air force found it buried in the WWII archives. Too bad you didn't think to use those connections, Viktoria."

She was too revved up to respond to the dig. "This is good, Feodyr. Very good."

Angling the phone, she switched to camera and took a shot before Chernak slammed her arm away. Rebel barely refrained from taking him down right then and there.

"Don't be stupid," she snarled. "The aerial map isn't any good by itself. But we can overlay it atop the mine schematic. See where bombs caved in the tunnels…"

"And where they didn't," Chernak finished on a rush. As excited now as she was, he refolded the map and stuffed it back in his pocket. "Anatoli! We will take your car. Nikolai, get the other American."

Rebel ignored Blade's thunderous expression when Nikolai thumped him between the shoulders and shoved him toward the apartment's door. She couldn't risk so much as a wink or a blink. He had to trust her, had to prevent that double agent remark from propagating all kinds of insidious doubts.

She draped her purse strap over her shoulder but kept her phone in hand. Before she followed Blade to the door, she took a last look at the kidnapped teenager. She hadn't moved. Her shoulders still sagged, her eyes still registered nothing but emptiness.

The girl's bruised face made Rebel ache to spin around and deliver a swift knick to Anatoli's nuts. She managed to constrain the impulse, but it gnawed at her insides as she trooped into the hall with Blade, Feodyr and Nikolai. They descended the stairs, then three of them hovered just inside the grimy door until Nikolai fetched Anatoli's tin can of a car from wherever it had been parked. Chernak made sure the street was clear before he sent the still-cuffed Blade out the door. He had to fold almost double to squeeze into the Mini's backseat.

Rebel was ordered into the front passenger seat. So Chernak could keep his weapon trained on her, she knew. While the Bulgarian crawled in beside Blade, she kept her eyes on the road ahead. She didn't give a clue to her intent as she thumbed her phone's keypad and reversed the no-comm signal. Nikolai put the car in gear while she was keying in a follow-on message to OMEGA control. As soon as it was done, she slipped the phone in her purse.

They turned a corner, traveled two blocks and took another turn before Rebel picked up the wail of sirens.

The wail grew louder, shrieking with urgency. Beside her Nikolai cursed and aimed an instinctive glance at the speedometer. A swift check of the rearview mirror showed Chernak tensing, as well. Neither man relaxed until four police cars sped by in the other lane, lights flashing and sirens screaming.

Rebel didn't move a single facial muscle. Inside, though, she was wearing a big honkin' grin. Tank had come through again. In a few minutes Hairy Harry would be on his way to a holding cell and the kidnapped girl would be wrapped in a blanket and on her way to safety.

Rebel's elation lasted until Nikolai pulled up outside a squat, featureless block of apartments on the outskirts of Kaliningrad. It was still warming her insides when he shoved the car into park, killed the ignition and disappeared inside one of the stairwells. He returned less than five minutes later with a laptop tucked under one arm. Sliding behind the wheel, he dumped the computer in Rebel's lap and queried his partner.

"Where do we go now?"

Chernak didn't hesitate. "Yantarny."

The teacup-size car rattled out of town and hit the wind- and sand-swept route to the coast a few minutes later. Without a storm or restless waves to churn up amber and lure day-trippers out from Kaliningrad, the two-lane road was pretty much deserted. They encountered exactly one car heading back into the city. None at all aiming for the sea.

The closer they got to the Baltic, the uneasier Rebel grew. Chewing on the inside of her lip, she eyed the desolate salt marshes and gray-hued dunes. Dammit! She should have insisted Chernak take them to an internet café in the city. Someplace with other people around. The bastard would've had to remove Blade's cuffs. Conceal his weapon. Act like they were just there to check email or the latest porn flicks. That would have given her five or ten seconds to maneuver. Now…

"Turn here."

Chernak's curt command had Nikolai swerving off the road and onto a rutted dirt track. When the track wound behind a sand dune, Rebel zinged a look in the rearview mirror. The tight cast to Chernak's face told her it was showtime.

Sure enough, Chernak ordered his pal to stop as soon as they were out of sight of the road. Her .38 appeared in the mirror a second later, the barrel leveled at the back of her head.

"Out of the car, Viktoria. You, too, *Amerikanski.* We will transfer the files to the computer here."

After which he would hold the gun to her head and force Blade to interpret the overlay. Or eliminate them both and take his chances on finding someone else who could do it for him. Rebel sincerely hoped it was the former but prepared for the latter.

She had her game plan worked out before she unscrewed her legs from under the dash. She exited the Mini, the laptop in hand. Her feet sank in sand. Brackish air filled her lungs. Blade got out awkwardly, his face set in stone.

Rebel made sure she maintained enough distance between them to keep Chernak focused primarily on her. At the same time, her now snapping senses registered Nikolai's every move on the far side of the vehicle. She had to assume he was armed, but she'd deal with that after she neutralized the Bulgarian now aiming the .38 at her middle.

"You've proved most useful, Viktoria." Chernak opted for English, obviously intending Blade to understand and be intimidated by every word. "I'm almost sorry our partnership has to end."

Rebel smiled and had the laptop ready to hurl when violent movement erupted to her right. She jerked around just in time to see Blade lunge at the Bulgarian, a loose cuff dangling from one wrist. She didn't wait for the results. Spinning the rest of the way around, she whipped the laptop across the top of the car and scored a direct hit on Nikolai's forehead.

Chapter 12

Rebel saw the laptop connect, watched Nikolai go down like a felled ox and spun back around. Chernak lay facedown in the dirt, out cold. Judging by the skinned and bloody knuckles on Blade's right hand, she guessed he would stay out for a while.

Gulping, she forced her heart out of her throat and back down into her chest before turning to check on Nikolai. The laptop had knocked him six ways to sideways. He was sprawled in a crumpled heap at the rear end of the car.

More shaken than she wanted to admit, Rebel turned back and watched Blade bend to retrieve her .38. The silver dangling from his wrist brought an involuntary exclamation.

"How'd you get out of the cuffs?"

"Escape and Evasion 101." The look he sent her wasn't friendly. "You miss that training session, Talbot?"

"No," she retorted, stung.

OMEGA's premier escape artist had taught operatives to pick any and every kind of lock with nothing more than a bobby pin. Rebel had been forced to point out that few females today stuck bobby pins in their hair. She'd also discovered that trick only worked if you had your hands in front of you and could use them to work the lock.

"Your arms were behind you," she said, still trying to figure out how he'd emulated Houdini. "And you didn't have your knife to pry them with."

"Yeah, about that…"

He rolled Chernak over and relieved him of the Marakov. Straightening, he tucked the second weapon in his waistband. He gave Nikolai a quick once-over before facing Rebel. His expression stony, he unbuckled his belt. Three seconds later the second cuff popped free.

"Damn!" She moved in for a closer look. "That's pretty slick. Maybe I should start wearing a belt when I'm in the field."

"Maybe you should."

Uh-oh. That flat, implacable tone told her she had to recover some serious ground. Essaying a smile, she held out a placating hand.

"I know you're pissed. Just give me a chance to…"

It happened so fast she didn't have time to jerk her hand back. In one blinding move, he snapped the cuff on her wrist, used her outstretched arm to twist her around, and shoved her against the car.

"C'mon, Black! Don't be an idiot!"

When he dragged her other arm behind her back, her first instinct was to retaliate with a swift backward kick. She curbed the response just in time. Heeling the man in the groin wasn't going to soothe his ruffled feathers. Hers, however, remained in full fluff while he went to relieve the still unconscious Nikolai of a small arsenal of weapons. Including, Rebel saw as she turned back around, his knife. The sharp, serrated bone blade gleamed a dull ivory when he walked back to her.

She looked from the knife to his face and felt a ripple of real fear. Defiantly, she lifted her chin. "You need to let me explain."

"You'll explain, all right. But first…"

When he brought the knife up, she couldn't help it. She flinched. And hated herself for it when he sliced through the shoulder strap of her purse.

"Bastard," she spit, as infuriated by her reaction as by his tight, mocking smile.

She sagged against the car while he extracted her phone. Since her comm device recognized only her biometrics, he couldn't key directly into a secure line. Instead, he had to manually dial a number and wait to be connected.

The number was a blind. It got him a chirpy receptionist for a twenty-four-hour floral house. Rebel followed along as Blade ordered two dozen red dahlias, was told they weren't in season, and placed a different order. Several oblique references later, he was patched through to OMEGA control. The comm techs on duty then performed a voice analysis to verify the caller before passing him on to the controller.

The whole process took twenty or thirty seconds at most. They were the longest damned thirty seconds Rebel could remember. Skewered by Blade's icy stare, she almost sighed in relief when he got through.

"Tank. Blade. Take a GPS lock on our position and get the police out here ASAP." He listened a moment. "That's right. Feodyr Chernak and one of his pals who goes by the name of Nikolai. Tell them Chernak is suspected of murdering Vivian Bauer and a curator at the Catherine Palace."

"Kurov," Rebel supplied, "Petr Kurov. And Chernak admitted both murders."

When Blade ignored her addendum, she sincerely regretted she hadn't swung a heel. Fuming, she listened to the one-sided conversation.

"They did?" He cocked a brow. "The girl's okay?"

The obvious reference to Anatoli's teenage sex slave took some of Rebel's heat. She had all of a moment or two of relief that the girl was safe before Blade's next remark got her steamed all over again.

"No, I can't." His flinty stare sliced into her. "I intend

to find out, though. Yeah, we'll stay on-scene. I'll give you an update after we finish with the police."

He cut the connection and shoved the phone in his back pocket. With his arms crossed and those weapons tucked in his waistband, he looked like some gunslinging gangster from the thirties.

"All right, Talbot. Talk."

Rebel had never believed that old cliché about seeing red. His arrogant stance and pigheaded demand made an instant believer out of her. Fury blazed hot, singed every part of her. He was her partner! Her lover! She'd broken every one of her self-imposed rules and tumbled into bed with him like some sex-starved nympho. True, that unexpected face-to-face with Chernak had left her scrambling. And yes, she'd fabricated layer upon layer of lies to find out what Feodyr knew. But she'd hissed at Blade to trust her. Was sure he would at least give her the benefit of the doubt.

Refusing to admit how deep his suspicion cut, she tilted her chin another notch. "Screw you, Black."

"What?"

His thundercloud of surprise afforded Rebel immense satisfaction. He hadn't expected defiance. Probably thought she would shiver and shake and beg him to listen. Not in this lifetime.

"You don't trust me? That's your problem, not mine."

"The hell it is."

She relaxed against the car, so angry and hurt she had

to work to maintain her sneer. "I'll wait till the cavalry arrives. We can sort things out then and…"

A low groan cut her off. Muttering an oath, Blade stalked to the rear of the car and manhandled a dazed but recovering Nikolai over to join his still out partner. An egg-size lump was already forming on Nikolai's forehead. Drawing up his knees, he cradled his head in both hands.

Blade kept both men in view without letting Rebel out of his line of sight. "Don't make this harder than it has to be," he snarled. "Clue me in, Talbot. What's your game?"

Stiff-necked pride brought her within a breath of telling him to go to hell again. Loyalty to OMEGA and a belated reminder of the importance of their mission made her grind out the truth.

"My first and only previous contact with Feodyr Chernak was in Moscow. I can't reveal the details but…"

Blade gave a low growl, which might have been pretty intimidating if she wasn't so angry herself. "That op is still classified! All you need to know is that it involved more than a million dollars worth of uncut heroin, not one ruble of which made it into the pockets of Chernak or of his bosses."

"Go on."

A stiff breeze gusted across the dunes, whipping her hair into a frenzy. She shook her head to get loose tendrils out of her eyes and forced herself to continue.

"I didn't know he was in Kaliningrad. And I had no idea he'd acquired a scar above his eyes. It's new, Blade. Not fully healed. You can see that as well as I can."

He refused to concede the point. Just looked at her with such suspicion that her fists bunched.

"I was as surprised as Feodyr was when we barreled into each other. I had to think fast. He and his bosses thought I'd used my military connections to help set up that heroin deal. So I had to convince Feodyr I'd left the military and gone rogue."

"Feodyr wasn't the only one you convinced."

That hurt. More than Rebel would allow him to see. Her voice went flat and cold. "He believed me enough to negotiate a deal. We traded information. He showed me what brought him to Kaliningrad, I told him…"

"You told him about Bauer's mission behind enemy lines?" Blade's face lit with fury. "Sicced that murdering bastard on the woman we talked to this afternoon?"

"No! Christ, just look at the phone!"

She stared him down. Not a real easy feat with the wind blowing her hair into her face and her shoulders now aching like nobody's business, but at last he yanked the phone out of his pocket again.

"Okay, I'm looking."

"Go to the saved files icon. Click on the last entry."

He did, not very enthusiastically. "It looks like some sort of topographical survey."

"That's exactly what it is. A WWII aerial reconnaissance photo of this area. One of Chernak's pals dug it out of the Russian air force's archives. Find the coast and zoom in on Yantarny."

Frowning, he used the directional buttons to move the photo around on the screen.

"Do you have it?" she asked impatiently.

"Yeah."

He looked up, skimmed a glance across the dunes all the way to the horizon, and went back to the screen. "It's not satellite quality but it's good," he conceded grudgingly, then with a little more animation, "Damned good."

"Okay, keep that file open and click on the second one."

"Looks like HTML code."

"Right. Just convert the…"

"I've got it."

He was already ahead of her, his thumbs working the keys with a dexterity a teenager would envy.

"Holy crap!"

"What?" Forgetting how pissed she was at him, Rebel pushed off the car. "Lemme see."

He hesitated just long enough for her to serious consider delivering that swift heel to the groin she'd contemplated earlier. Then slowly, reluctantly, he angled the screen around.

Rebel had studied enough aerial reconnaissance maps during her air force years to instantly identify the topographical features of the Yantarny Mine area. The sweeping coastline washed by waves. The undulating dunes. The vast, gray crater. Only instead of rusting, abandoned equipment, this photo showed two active dredges in the process of scooping sludge from the underground table. And a faint line in the earth! Hardly more than a bump. But the shadowy line corresponded exactly with the schematic overlay showing a rail spur leading from the mine in the direction of Königsberg.

"Blade! It's just what we thought! That tunnel must have…"

She caught herself and threw a quick look at the other two. Nikolai still sat with his heads in his hands. Chernak was just coming awake. His legs twitched a couple of times, and a moment later his eyes blinked open. He stared up at the sky, obviously trying to clear the cobwebs.

Blade offered assistance. Tucking the phone back in his pocket, he leveled the Marakov at the two men. "Hey! Asshole! Over here."

Chernak propped himself up on one elbow and put a hand to his jaw, wincing as he moved it from side to side. His furious gaze locked on Rebel, now cuffed instead of Blade.

This was good, she realized instantly. The Bulgarian obviously thought Blade considered her one of the bad guys. Which he did, unfortunately, but she would straighten that out later. Right now she could see all kinds of possibilities if Chernak and his bosses believed she was, in fact, a rogue agent. She was envisioning the undercover ops she might work in that guise when the Feodyr issued a low threat.

"You will be sorry for this, *Amerikanski*."

"Tell that to the cavalry. They'll be here any moment."

Chernak looked so blank Rebel had to translate. "He means the police. The *oblast*."

The Bulgarian sucked in a breath. "He called the *oblast*? The Kaliningrad *oblast*?"

Not exactly, but she wasn't about to explain the call had been relayed by a supersecret agency of the U.S. government Chernak had never heard of and didn't need to know existed. Still, she didn't like the way Feodyr's face closed down. He just went blank. Completely empty. As if he didn't want to give her—or Blade—even a vague clue to what he was thinking.

That sudden shutdown started a dozen uneasy thoughts racing through her mind. Foremost among them was the fact that Kaliningrad carried the reputation of being a wide-open city. Guns, drugs, white slaves. All available for the right price. Even Clara Soloff had mentioned that half the police took bribes.

On the other hand...

The police had raided Anatoli's apartment and rescued the kidnapped girl. Blade's comments during his conversation with Tank had verified as much. Unless she'd misinterpreted his end of the conversation. Had OMEGA merely confirmed that the police were responding, without knowing the final outcome?

Suddenly and intensely worried, she tried to figure out how to convey her concerns without alerting Chernak. She was still trying when the sounds of engines carried over the wind and distant sea.

She listened a moment, then felt her stomach sink like a stone. Those were engines. Not sirens. And they were coming fast.

"Clint! We have to get out of here. Now!"

"What?"

"Do you hear those vehicles? They're not the police."

"How the hell do you…?"

He broke off. Cocked his head. Registered the absence of sirens.

They could see the plumes of dust swirled up by the speeding cars now. The vehicles were still a couple miles away but closing fast. Her pulse racing, Rebel assessed their options. Climbing back into the Mini wouldn't get them anywhere. Sand dunes blocked any forward movement. By the time they backed the car down the track and hit the main road, the approaching vehicles would have reached the turnoff. She turned to Blade, saw he'd made the same grim assessment. Aided, she guessed, by the feral smile now creasing Chernak's face.

"We've got to get out of here," she repeated urgently. "But I can't run like this. Unlock the cuffs!"

In that sharp, crystalline instant she knew her future with Clink Black hung by a thread. Would he trust her? Or would he think this was another of her devious ploys?

She felt a vein throb in her temple. Tension churned in her stomach. She should have told him, she thought desperately. Last night, when he'd pinned her against the wall and driven her wild. This morning, when she'd straddled his hips and returned the favor. She should have told him then that he'd erased her last, lingering regret over her botched marriage. Should have admitted she'd shed her irritation over his come-hither grin. Craved it, in fact. Too late to tell him now, though. She'd missed her chance.

"Turn around."

The curt command didn't exactly spell hearts and flowers, but Rebel nearly whooped with relief. She did as he instructed, careful not to put herself between him and the other two. Incredibly, he managed to spring the cuffs with one hand while keeping Chernak and pal covered with the other. When they got out of this mess, she thought wryly, he *had* to show her how he did that.

"Hook their ankles together."

She complied, being careful to avoid a grab or kick from either man. The moment she had them shackled together, she and Blade took off.

They had a four- or five-minute start at most.

Running full steam, they plowed over a series of low dunes anchored by scrub brush and clumps of tough, silvery grass. The sand was hard packed and more gray than brown from the decades of sludge the Yantarny mine had dumped into the sea. Rebel couldn't bring herself to regret all that poisonous pollution at the moment. At least she and Blade weren't having to wallow through soft white powder They might just make it to the faded resort town of Yantarny and find some safety in numbers.

Her brief burst of optimism sputtered and died when they topped a mound that gave them an unbroken vista of the Baltic. The resort beckoned in the distance. Too far in the distance, she saw in dismay. She and Blade would make prime targets if they tried to cross another mile or more of landscape covered with nothing but low scrub and wind-whipped grass. To her immense relief, Blade had already come up with Plan B.

"That aerial reconnaissance photo," he said, snatching the phone from his pocket again. "I only got a glimpse of it but I think… I'm sure…"

When he slowed to work the on-screen image, she threw a quick look over her shoulder. She could see the speeding vehicles clearly now. They'd almost reached the turnoff to the dirt track. What she didn't see were any distinctive insignia. Her last faint hope they might be unmarked police vehicles died when she spotted Feodyr and Nikolai running an awkward, three-legged race for the main road, arms locked around each other's waists and their free hands waving madly in the air.

Gulping, she tried to speed up the pace. "We're going to have company pretty quick."

Blade jogged alongside, still working the screen. "I know I saw it."

"Saw what?"

"A hole. I'm thinking it may be a cave-in."

She didn't like the sound of that "may." In a fever of impatience, she peered over his arm to see the area he was searching but their forward movement made everything on the screen a blur from her angle.

"It should be… Yes! Here it is!" He whipped his head up, took a fix on their location and veered off at an angle. "This way."

They raced across another fifty yards of dunes with Rebel looking over her shoulder every few steps. She saw Chernak and Nikolai run out onto the main road. Saw the approaching vehicles skid to a stop. Saw four men emerge. Four heavily armed men, none of whom wore uniforms. Then, fortunately or un-, she and Blade plunged down the slope of a tall dune that cut off her view of Chernak and company.

Only it wasn't a dune, she saw when she half scooted, half slid into the depression. It was a bowl of hard-packed earth overgrown with weeds and sawgrass. Thankful she was wearing jeans, she got up, ready to run again, but Blade had stopped to take another fix.

"GPS says this is it. The exact spot of the cave-in."

Straining to hear any sound of pursuit, Rebel surveyed the immediate area. She saw nothing promising while Blade paced to the right, turned left, then right again.

She didn't dare poke her head above the lip of the bowl. She wanted to, though. She hunched her shoulders in anticipation of an imminent shout, a shot and the slam of a bullet. She'd was about to tell Blade to give it up when he shoved the phone in his back pocket again and dropped to one knee in front of a clump of tall, silvery grass.

Mother Nature knew what she was doing when she gave these coastal grasses such long, intractable roots. They had to go down deep to anchor the dunes and keep them from blowing away when storms howled in from the sea. But Mother Nature's roots were no match for a tough, determined male with at least one cold-blooded killer and five other goons on his tail.

Planting a foot against the sloping mound, Blade wrapped both hands around the plant's base. It took several grunts, a vicious curse and three sweating, straining pulls before the grass gave up the fight. The roots tore loose, almost landing Blade on his butt. He recovered just in time and tossed the clump aside to peer into the small, dark hole he'd ripped in the earth.

Or not so small!

Too late he realized dislodging the plant had also dislodged the softer dirt below. It now crumbled beneath his feet. A few clods at first, then, before he could leap aside, the whole damned thing collapsed. Wearing an almost comical expression of surprise, Blade dropped out of sight.

Chapter 13

"Blade!"

Dropping to all fours, Rebel crawled toward the gaping hole. Her heart stopped when the dirt under one hand crumbled, then started again with a painful kick when another tuft of grass kept the hole from widening and sucking her in, too.

She peered over the edge, terrified she would see a black, bottomless pit. Or the top of Blade's head sinking into a pool of viscous gray sludge. The sight of him dusting himself off and looking around a subterranean chamber of some sort made her go limp with relief.

"Are you okay?"

He tipped his head and flashed her a look of fierce

satisfaction. "Better than okay. I see rail tracks. Looks like we found the spur."

"No kidding!"

"Drop down," he called. "I'll catch you. Bring the clump of grass I dug up with you."

"Huh?"

"You can stand on my shoulders and plug the hole. It might buy us some time."

"Oh. Right."

She grabbed the uprooted plant and switched from a doggie crawl to a squat. Now all she had to do was scoot around and tip over. Like in that dumb exercise where you were supposed to fall back and let your partner catch you. Just because she and Blade were having slight trust issues at the moment was no reason to think he'd let her land on her head. Still she did a mental finger cross as she angled around and toppled backward.

She landed in his arms with a shower of dirt and her fistful of grass. Giddy with relief, she looked up into his face and suddenly, stupidly, all was right with the world again. The suspicion had disappeared from his eyes. His grin was back, and it sent Rebel into another crazy tumble.

"When we get back to civilization," she heard herself say, "remind me to tell you that I love you."

His startled expression was even more comical this time than when he'd dropped feetfirst into the hole.

"If we didn't have Chernak and friends breathing

down our neck," she said, laughing, "I'd show you how much."

He recovered fast. Shedding his surprise, he let her slide to her feet. "I'll settle for a short demo."

And short it was. A hard, fast fusion of lips and bodies. And hearts! She could feel his accelerating against her chest. Feel hers speeding up to match him beat for beat. The ridiculous idea of making love in a dark, dank hole jumped into her head. The possibility of an entire colony of bats horning in on the action shoved it out again.

"Okay." Blade pushed her away, breathing hard. "We need to plug that hole."

They soon discovered plugging it was a whole lot trickier than making it. He got her on his shoulders and clamped fists around her ankles but every time he tried to push out of the crouch, she lost her balance. Finally he moved to the dirt wall, had her climb aboard, and inched toward the hole with Rebel steadying herself by flattening her free hand against the roof. She didn't want to even *think* about what her palm encountered on its way to the opening. Some of it was earthy. Some of it was damp. The slimy parts she blocked out of her mind.

She concealed the hole as best she could and resisted the impulse to attempt a Lara Croft, "Tomb Raider"-style somersault off his shoulders. Once on her feet, she finally had a chance to look around. Just enough light filtered through the hastily plugged hole to confirm this was, in fact, a man-made chamber. A storage area was positioned along the rail spur, if those stacked barrels and canvas-shrouded stacks were any indication. The white letters stenciled on the barrels snagged her instant attention.

"That print is in German, not Russian! This cache must be prewar, when this was still East Prussia."

"Or stashed here in the last days of the war," Blade concurred.

The possibility one of those canvas tarps might conceal twenty-six hastily packed crates closed Rebel's throat. "Do you think they're here? The Amber Room panels."

"Only one way to find out."

He yanked off a tarp and sent a cloud of thick gray dust swirling through the dim cavern. Rebel sneezed and crowded closer, only to grunt in disappointment at the sight of neatly stacked pipes. A second tarp produced stacks of rusting metal rings ranging in diameter from one to five or six feet.

"Clamps," Blade murmured. "Used to piece together hose sections."

The hoses themselves—or what was left of them—lay in disintegrating coils under a third tarp. The barrels contained gasoline, no doubt used to power the dredges.

"Well, hell." Her excitement fading, Rebel scanned the uncovered items. "Looks like it's all mine equipment."

"We've still got the tunnel to explore. We might find something farther down the rail line."

She eyed the rusting tracks with something less than enthusiasm. A solid wall of earth from the cave-in blocked the tracks in one direction. Black, unrelieved emptiness swallowed them in the other.

"We need to check under the rest of the tarps," Blade said. "We might find some candles or lanterns. If not, we can rig torches and soak them in the gasoline."

They didn't find a lantern but the last covering Rebel twitched off made her gasp. "Look at this!"

"This" was a 1940s-era German military motorcycle, complete with sidecar and rifle mount.

"It's a Zundapp KS 750," she exclaimed, "designed at specific request of the German army. This baby could cruise at eighty kilometers per hour or creep at less than three alongside marching troops. It came with a preheating element so troops on the Russian front could start its 750cc engine even in subzero temperatures. Or it did," she added dubiously as she moved around the sidecar and got her first glimpse of the bike's gutted frame.

Instead of an engine, this particular Zundapp sported chains, pulleys and pedals. And some sadistic soul had replaced the rubber wheels with railcar type wheels—two on the frame side, one supporting the side car.

"Oh, no!" Rebel mourned. "They made a damned tricycle out of it."

"Could be it wasn't safe to run a gasoline-powered engine underground with no way to vent the fumes,"

Blade pointed out. "They probably had to jerry-rig vehicles like this to get back and forth from town."

"I guess."

The Zundapp's mutilation was almost as painful for her as finding no trace of the Amber Room panels. Her only consolation was that a thin chain led from the multigear sprocket to what looked like a small generator attached to the bike's headlight.

Anxious to test her speculation that the pedaling might power the lamp, Blade hefted one end of the bastardized vehicle.

"Let's get this baby on the rails."

Rebel resigned herself to descending from the ranks of biker chic to scooter bitch and hefted the other. Gutted of most of its innards, the motorcycle and its attached sidecar were easily manhandled onto the tracks.

Getting them moving proved even easier. Too easy, in fact. When Rebel swung into the saddle, her weight provided sufficient tractional engagement that one stand on the pedals sent the contraption zinging forward.

"Whoa!"

She applied the handbrakes instinctively, then realized there *weren't* any handbrakes. Muttering, she dropped back on the seat and backpedaled just in time to avoid slamming into the earth blocking one end of the tunnel. She reversed direction, pedaling more slowly this time, and yelped in delight when the headlamp began to glow. Okay, so maybe whoever had cannibalized the Zundapp didn't do such a bad reengineering job after all.

She brought the bike to a halt beside Blade and grinned. "Climb aboard."

"You sure you can manage the additional weight?" he asked, eyeing the sidecar speculatively.

She'd figured out the physics now. The more weight they applied to the rails, the more traction they would generate.

"I can handle it."

The sidecar presented almost as much of a challenge as Anatoli's Mini. Once Blade had wedged himself in, Rebel stood on the pedals again. Two grunts later she had them heading for the black hole at the far end of the storage site.

Her exuberance faded more the deeper they got into the tunnel. The bike's headlamp proved totally ineffective against the Stygian gloom. The puny beam penetrated barely ten or twelve yards ahead. The air got heavy, too. Heavy and dank and earthy, as though it hadn't been replenished in fifty or sixty years. Not a good omen, Rebel thought. Odds were they wouldn't find an escape route wherever this tunnel ended.

Worse, she could swear she heard subterranean creatures scurrying out of their way. What, besides bats, lived in this inky darkness? she wondered uneasily. Rats? Moles? Centipedes devoid of all pigmentation after millennia of nesting deep in caves? The idea some pale pink or dead-white troglodyte might glom onto her leg or drop down on her head had her so rattled she didn't notice the solid black bulk looming directly ahead.

"Watch out!"

Blade's shout had her standing on the pedals. She slowed their forward momentum, thank God, but they both put up their arms to protect themselves from the wall that came rushing at them.

No, not a wall, she saw when the Zundapp whispered to a halt mere inches from what looked like a railroad boxcar. The damned thing was just sitting there, abandoned in the middle of the tunnel. Or not...

The possibility it might have been parked there deliberately occurred to Rebel the same moment it did to Blade.

"Omigod," she breathed. "This could be the one. The last boxcar out of Königsberg."

"Could be," he echoed, every bit as jazzed as she was.

She almost fell off the bike in her haste to dismount while Blade levered himself out of the sidecar. She said a quick prayer that she'd fed the headlamp enough juice to keep it alive while they checked out the boxcar. Those faint scurries had left an indelible impression on her psyche.

Blade reached the boxcar's side panel first. Rebel was right on his heels. The industrial size padlock on the sliding panel elicited her fervent wish that they'd searched the storehouse area for a crowbar.

"Not a problem." Coolly, he extracted the Marakov from his waistband. "This might take a couple of shots," he warned. "They could ricochet. You'd better take cover on the other side of the boxcar."

"Oh, sure! Like I'm going to leave you to dodge bullets."

"Don't be stupid. Take cover."

"Did I not make myself clear?" Irritated, she planted herself between him and the padlock. "I love you. Lest you think that's a trivial declaration, you're only the fourth male I've said it to in my entire life."

"Fourth?" His brows snapped together. "I thought…"

"My grandfather on my mom's side," she cut in ruthlessly. "My dad. My ex. Now you. Do *not* make me go for five."

Laughter wiped out his frown. Taking care to keep the Marakov's barrel angled away, he hooked his other arm around her waist. A quick tug spilled her against his chest.

"If it makes you feel any better, you're on my short list."

Her breath caught. Had she read this right? Was he saying he loved her? Feeling uncharacteristically and ridiculously insecure, she had to ask.

"How short?"

"I never knew one grandmother and the other was the grandmother from hell. So that leaves my mom, who I'm embarrassed to admit I never actually said the words to."

Surprise, surprise. She was just thinking that a handsome charmer like Clint Black must have developed considerable skill at dodging the dreaded *L* word when he cupped her face.

"So you're the first, Victoria. I love you. Beats the hell out of me why, but I do."

Oooookay. It didn't exactly constitute a world-class declaration. But when he dropped a hard, fast kiss on her mouth, she decided it would do. Very nicely, in fact.

"Now go take cover."

Since she didn't see an alternative, she rounded the end of the boxcar. It was a tight fit, less than six inches between the car and the tunnel's earthen wall. Rebel edged sideways and sucked in her gut. Two steps later she let out a shout.

"Blade! This side's open!"

He joined in five seconds flat. Unfortunately, when he squeezed in beside her he completely blocked the headlamp's weak, diffused glow. Rebel refused to climb into that pitch-black boxcar blind.

"Back out," she instructed Blade. "You're blocking the light."

He complied, but still she hesitated. God only knew what kind of critters had taken up residence inside. She sidled to the opening, leaned forward a scant inch or two, peered into the inky interior. Gradually, her eyes adjusted.

"It's empty," she reported, swamped by waves of disappointment. "Completely, totally em— Wait! There's something in the corner. Looks like a crate."

"Only one?"

"Only one," she confirmed.

That pretty much killed the chances that they'd found the missing Amber Room panels. Thoroughly bummed, Rebel leaned in a little farther.

"It's got writing on it. Big, handwritten letters in white paint. 'Kil' something."

"Kaliningrad?"

"No."

She made out *K-I-L-R-O* but couldn't read the final letter of that first word. She didn't have to. The rest of the phrase said it all. Whooping, she wedged back to where Blade waited with a question written all over his face.

"Kilroy," she told him, grinning. "It says 'Kilroy was here, March '45.'"

"I'll be damned!"

As a former army grunt, he was as familiar with the classic bit of WWII graffiti as Rebel. American G.I.'s had scrawled the phrase on any and every imaginable surface, usually just below a cartoon showing the nose and bald head of a figure peeking over a wall. Reportedly, German intelligence had noted Kilroy on so many pieces of captured American equipment that they thought it was code for a top level spy. And Stalin had supposedly asked aides who the devil Kilroy was when he found the same graffiti on a wall in the VIP bathroom during the Potsdam Conference.

"My money's on Thomas Bauer," Rebel said, excited by the fact they'd solved at least this piece of the puzzle. "I bet you anything he found this boxcar stashed away here in the tunnel."

Blade matched her grin. "That would be my guess, too. There couldn't have been many other American G.I.s running loose in Königsberg in March 1945."

"We need to go back to the supply dump and make one of those torches you talked about. I want to see what's inside that crate."

She'd already resigned herself to the probability that it *didn't* contain even one of the missing amber panels. The original panels were too big, too heavy, to fit inside the box she'd spotted. But the crate could hold a smaller piece. A section from the Spring panel, perhaps. Or just the original rose medallion that Bauer had extracted his souvenir from. Lost in the possibilities, she didn't notice Blade had come to a dead stop beside the Zundapp until she plowed into him.

"What…?"

He sliced a hand through the air to cut her off and pitched his voice to a low murmur. "We've got company."

Leaning around him, she saw the thin, distant spear of a flashlight. "Feodyr and friends. Crap!"

The light was still just a pinprick in the darkness.

And the Zundapp's lamp was pointed away from them. There was a chance they hadn't yet spotted its dim glow.

Blade had obviously been thinking along the same lines. He twisted, found the wire connecting the pedal-powered generator, tore it loose, and plunged them into smothering, suffocating darkness.

"We'll see them before they see us," he whispered in her ear. "We'll have to maximize that advantage."

Some advantage, Rebel thought as she shut her mind to all thoughts of nasty night creatures and focused on the problem at hand.

"You go right and climb into the boxcar," Blade murmured. "I'll take the left side of the tunnel."

"That's it?" she whispered. "That's your plan? I go right, you go left?"

"You got a better one?" he shot back. "I'm wide-open to suggestions here."

"I *suggest* you give me my .38."

There was a moment of stark silence. The slam of it hit Rebel like a two-by-four. Oh, God! He still didn't trust her! She was fighting to clear what felt like a throat laced with glass shards when he chuckled.

"Sorry. I forgot I had it. Here."

He took her elbow and guided her hand. The familiar feel of cross-hatched steel hit her palm. Then his loose hold moved up her arm until his fingers found her chin and tipped her face to his.

"Remember," he murmured. "You're the first, Victoria. The first, and the only."

All she could see was the faint gleam of his eyes. And, incredibly, the white of his teeth as he grinned down at her.

"When we get out of here, we'll make it official."

She decided this wasn't the time to demand minor details. Like what, exactly, he meant by *official.* Especially when he followed that with a kiss and a low command.

"Just keep your head down."

"Ditto."

He threw a glance at the light spear still far down the tunnel and tightened his grip on her chin. "If you…"

He broke off, his body tensing, and Rebel felt her veins ice over.

"What?" she whispered.

"It's my phone. The thing's vibrating like hell."

"Well, for God's sake, answer it!"

Tank. It had to be Tank. Or Dodge. Or Lightning. Or one of the comm techs. Mentally reciting an entire litany of possibilities, Rebel conceded there wasn't a damned thing anyone in OMEGA could do at this point. She and Blade had waited too long. They'd put all their effort into eluding pursuit, then the thrill of the hunt. Now they would pay the price.

"Yeah, it's me," Blade muttered into the phone. "No. No."

The terse negatives were followed by another moment of stark silence, not quite as painful for Rebel as the last one but still pretty daunting. She eyed the bobbing light beam and had to bite back the urgent demand to know who the hell he was talking to. Stewing with impatience, she heard him ask only one question.

"You're sure?"

Her nerves were screaming when he slapped the phone back in his pocket.

"That was Tank," Blade confirmed. "He's been tracking our every step."

"And?"

"And he had our contact in Moscow alert every cop, city official and street sweeper in Kaliningrad and Yantarny. An entire regiment reportedly converged on the scene topside just minutes after we departed it. Tank said they engaged in a real Wild-West style shoot-out."

"And?"

"Chernak and his pals went down. Those are the good guys back there in the tunnel, searching for us."

Wave upon wave of relief crashed through Rebel. Every part of her itched with the need to get out of the creepy darkness. And yet…

She had to admit this underground interlude had spawned some *very* interesting moments. The question now was how much of what she and Blade had shared down here would survive the light of day.

Chapter 14

Despite having been organized in less than three days, the reception to announce the return of Russia's long-lost treasures would have delighted Peter the Great himself.

The palace named for his beloved wife Catherine preened in all its Baroque glory. Floodlights illuminated the 14-karat gold leaf on the onion domes of the palace's chapel. Every window in the ornate, seemingly mile-long facade glowed with the light from glittering chandeliers and candelabra. A military band wearing tall shakos and eighteenth-century uniforms welcomed guests with rousing Russian marches. Footmen in powdered wigs and tight knee breeches escorted the gowned and tuxedoed VIPs up the palace's magnificent central staircase. In the dazzling, brilliantly lit Hall of Mirrors, more footmen circulated with silver trays of champagne while a string orchestra filled the hall with lilting selections from Tchaikovsky, Borodin and Rimsky-Korsakov.

Nick and Mackenzie Jensen had flown over for the occasion. So had Maggie and Adam Ridgeway. They weren't about to miss seeing their son decorated by the Russian government. The same son, Adam had reminded his wife drily, they'd had to bail out of a Mexican jail at the age of ten and royally ream out after an unfortunate incident involving his fifth-grade social studies teacher and the bad-tempered iguana Maggie had kept as a pet.

"There he is now," Adam said, tipping his champagne flute to the tall, confident man his scamp of a son had become.

He wouldn't have chosen a career as an undercover operative for Tank, any more than he'd wanted his daughter Gillian to work even temporarily with OMEGA. He knew all too well the dangers involved. Yet under his pleated white shirt, Adam's chest swelled with pride at having his son follow in his footsteps. If not for the woman standing beside him, he might even have envied Tank the years ahead.

He slanted a glance at his wife. Maggie wore her light brown hair up, caught with the diamond clip he'd given her for Christmas last year. Baby-fine tendrils curled at her nape and stirred an instant need to nuzzle.

All these years, Adam thought ruefully, and the woman still made his mind swim. He couldn't indulge in any nuzzling at the moment but he could—and did—lean in and drop a discreet kiss on her temple.

Tilting her head, she smiled up at him. "What was that for?"

"Because you're you."

He would have said more if not for Nick's smirk, Mackenzie's grin and his son's arrival.

"Have you seen Victoria or Clint?" Tank asked.

"No," Nick answered. "We thought they were driving out in the limo with you."

"That was the plan. But Clint called my hotel room and said something had come up."

His four listeners switched instantly into OMEGA mode. Thunder and Chameleon might be retired from active service and Mac consulted only on an ad hoc basis these days, but they knew as well as Lightning that neither Rebel nor Blade would offend the Russian government by voluntarily skipping this ceremony.

The premier himself was here to view the masterpieces recovered from the underground tunnel. There were five in the crate, all lost in the chaos immediately preceding the brutal 900-day siege of St. Petersburg. Two Rembrandts, a landscape by Tintoretto, a still life by Jan Fyt and a portrait of Tsar Alexander in full dress uniform. The supposition now was that curators had missed the crate during their frenzy to pack and remove Catherine Palace's treasures ahead of the advancing German army.

That Germans had subsequently shipped the crate to Prussia along with the original Amber Room panels was more than mere supposition, however. Catherine Palace's director, Vassily Mikailovitch, had himself verified the authenticity of the amber rose tucked in the corner of the box. The world might never know what happened to the gem-studded panels the rose had come from but that piece, at least, had been restored to its original place and was ready for viewing.

A fact underscored by Mikailovitch and the towering figure accompanying him. None of the OMEGA crew acknowledged that they knew bull-like Anton Gorsky in anything other than his role as a low-ranking official in Russia's Ministry of Culture, but Lightning was sure he caught a flicker of concern behind Gorsky's otherwise impassive mask.

"The premier should arrive soon," Mikailovitch said to Tank, obviously worried. "We must get you, Mr. Ridgeway and your associates in place. Will you tell them, please?"

"I will, as soon as… Oh, good! Here they are."

Seven relieved people swung to face the two now weaving through the glittering crowd. Blade looked smooth and sophisticated in his hand-tailored tux. He also, they noted with considerable interest, kept a proprietary hand at the small of Rebel's back.

She snared second and third looks from every male

present, including Nick and both Ridgeways. They'd worked with her in suits, in jeans and tanks, in hip-hugging leathers. None of them had seen her draped in a gown of shimmering gold split to midthigh, however, much less sporting an amber pendant the size of a half-dollar. It hung from a velvet ribbon tied around her throat and glistened with her every step.

"Sorry we're late," she apologized breathlessly. "I, uh, got tangled up in something and couldn't get away."

"It does not matter," Mikailovitch lied, not very convincingly. "You are here now. Come, I will show you to your place."

He took her arm and led the way. Tank and Blade turned to follow, but Lightning stopped them before they'd taken more than a step.

"Hold on."

He strolled up to Blade and reached for the half circle of steel just showing under the hem of his tuxedo jacket. Palming the cuffs, he slipped them into his own pocket.

"I don't think you need these."

"Not until after the ceremony," Blade agreed. "I'm trying to teach Victoria how to spring 'em," he explained solemnly. "I figure she might get the hang of it by our silver wedding anniversary."

All eyes went to the woman now struggling to hold back her laughter.

"I wouldn't bet on it," she said, grinning. "I can be a *real* slow learner when I want to."

* * * * *

ROMANTIC SUSPENSE

COMING NEXT MONTH

Available August 30, 2011

You can find more information on upcoming
Harlequin® titles, free excerpts and more at
www.HarlequinInsideRomance.com.

REQUEST YOUR FREE BOOKS!
2 FREE NOVELS PLUS 2 FREE GIFTS!

 Harlequin®

ROMANTIC
SUSPENSE
Sparked by Danger, Fueled by Passion.

YES! Please send me 2 FREE Harlequin® Romantic Suspense novels and my 2 FREE gifts (gifts are worth about $10). After receiving them, if I don't wish to receive any more books, I can return the shipping statement marked "cancel." If I don't cancel, I will receive 4 brand-new novels every month and be billed just $4.49 per book in the U.S. or $5.24 per book in Canada. That's a saving of at least 14% off the cover price! It's quite a bargain! Shipping and handling is just 50¢ per book in the U.S. and 75¢ per book in Canada.* I understand that accepting the 2 free books and gifts places me under no obligation to buy anything. I can always return a shipment and cancel at any time. Even if I never buy another book, the two free books and gifts are mine to keep forever.

240/340 HDN FEFR

Name	(PLEASE PRINT)
Address	Apt. #
City	State/Prov. Zip/Postal Code

Signature (if under 18, a parent or guardian must sign)

Mail to the **Reader Service:**
IN U.S.A.: P.O. Box 1867, Buffalo, NY 14240-1867
IN CANADA: P.O. Box 609, Fort Erie, Ontario L2A 5X3

Not valid for current subscribers to Harlequin Romantic Suspense books.

Want to try two free books from another line?
Call 1-800-873-8635 or visit www.ReaderService.com.

* Terms and prices subject to change without notice. Prices do not include applicable taxes. Sales tax applicable in N.Y. Canadian residents will be charged applicable taxes. Offer not valid in Quebec. This offer is limited to one order per household. All orders subject to credit approval. Credit or debit balances in a customer's account(s) may be offset by any other outstanding balance owed by or to the customer. Please allow 4 to 6 weeks for delivery. Offer available while quantities last.

Your Privacy—The Reader Service is committed to protecting your privacy. Our Privacy Policy is available online at www.ReaderService.com or upon request from the Reader Service.

We make a portion of our mailing list available to reputable third parties that offer products we believe may interest you. If you prefer that we not exchange your name with third parties, or if you wish to clarify or modify your communication preferences, please visit us at www.ReaderService.com/consumerschoice or write to us at Reader Service Preference Service, P.O. Box 9062, Buffalo, NY 14269. Include your complete name and address.

HRS11B

New York Times *and* USA TODAY *bestselling author*
Maya Banks presents a brand-new miniseries

PREGNANCY & PASSION

When four irresistible tycoons face
the consequences of temptation.

Book 1—ENTICED BY HIS FORGOTTEN LOVER

Available September 2011 from Harlequin® Desire®!

Rafael de Luca had been in bad situations before. A crowded ballroom could never make him sweat.

These people would never know that he had no memory of any of them.

He surveyed the party with grim tolerance, searching for the source of his unease.

At first his gaze flickered past her, but he yanked his attention back to a woman across the room. Her stare bored holes through him. Unflinching and steady, even when his eyes locked with hers.

Petite, even in heels, she had a creamy olive complexion. A wealth of inky-black curls cascaded over her shoulders and her eyes were equally dark.

She looked at him as if she'd already judged him and found him lacking. He'd never seen her before in his life. Or had he?

He cursed the gaping hole in his memory. He'd been diagnosed with selective amnesia after his accident four months ago. Which seemed like complete and utter bull. No one got amnesia except hysterical women in bad soap operas.

With a smile, he disengaged himself from the group

around him and made his way to the mystery woman.

She wasn't coy. She stared straight at him as he approached, her chin thrust upward in defiance.

"Excuse me, but have we met?" he asked in his smoothest voice.

His gaze moved over the generous swell of her breasts pushed up by the empire waist of her black cocktail dress.

When he glanced back up at her face, he saw fury in her eyes.

"Have we *met?*" Her voice was barely a whisper, but he felt each word like the crack of a whip.

Before he could process her response, she nailed him with a right hook. He stumbled back, holding his nose.

One of his guards stepped between Rafe and the woman, accidentally sending her to one knee. Her hand flew to the folds of her dress.

It was then, as she cupped her belly, that the realization hit him. She was pregnant.

Her eyes flashing, she turned and ran down the marble hallway.

Rafael ran after her. He burst from the hotel lobby, and saw two shoes sparkling in the moonlight, twinkling at him.

He blew out his breath in frustration and then shoved the pair of sparkly, ultrafeminine heels at his head of security.

"Find the woman who wore these shoes."

Will Rafael find his mystery woman?
Find out in Maya Banks's passionate new novel
ENTICED BY HIS FORGOTTEN LOVER
Available September 2011 from Harlequin® Desire®!

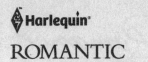

Harlequin®

ROMANTIC
SUSPENSE

NEW YORK TIMES BESTSELLING AUTHOR
RACHEL LEE

The Rescue Pilot

Time is running out...

Desperate to help her ailing sister, Rory is determined
to get Cait the necessary treatment to help her fight
a devastating disease. A cross-country trip turns into
a fight for survival in more ways than one when their plane
encounters trouble. Can Rory trust pilot Chase Dakota
with their lives, and possibly her heart?

**Look for this heart-stopping romance in September
from *New York Times* bestselling author Rachel Lee
and Harlequin Romantic Suspense!**

Available in September wherever books are sold!

www.Harlequin.com.

RSRL27741